The Watermelon King

BOOKS BY DANIEL WALLACE

Big Fish

Ray in Reverse

The Watermelon King

The
Watermelon King

Daniel Wallace

HOUGHTON MIFFLIN COMPANY

Boston   New York   2003

Copyright © 2003 by Daniel Wallace

For information about permission to reproduce
selections from this book, write to Permissions,
Houghton Mifflin Company, 215 Park Avenue South,
New York, New York 10003.

Visit our Web site: www.houghtonmifflinbooks.com.

Library of Congress Cataloging-in-Publication Data
Wallace, Daniel, date.
The Watermelon King / Daniel Wallace.
p. cm.
ISBN 0-618-22138-7
1. Grandfathers—Death—Fiction. 2. Maternal depri-
vation—Fiction. 3. Watermelon industry—Fiction.
4. Young men—Fiction. 5. Alabama—Fiction. I. Title.
PS3573.A4256348 W35 2003
813'.54—dc21 2002075941

Book design by Melissa Lotfy
Typefaces: Bembo and Barcelona

Printed in the United States of America

DOC 10 9 8 7 6 5 4 3 2 1

For Laura

ACKNOWLEDGMENTS

Thanks go to the following people for reading this book through its many incarnations: Holland Wallace, Barrie Wallace, Abby Tripp, Lillian Bayley, Ellen Lefcourt, Patty Kadel, Carol Hickman, Erika Krouse, Howard Sanders, and Richard Green; to Laura Wallace, first reader, whose name changed while I was writing this book, but whose sweet heart didn't; to Joe Regal, whose continued faith in me is reassuring but somewhat puzzling; to Heidi Pitlor, who made this a much better book; and especially to Alan Shapiro, whose friendship, cool head, and keen eye were invaluable.

ONE

*T*he town emerged a few miles past the freeway exit, its rooftops and church spires just visible above a long, thick stand of pine. An abandoned cinder-block gas station, antique and dilapidated, its pumps rusted and brown, stood forlorn at the city limits, grass shoots growing through the cracked concrete as though it were soil. The door to the station itself had been removed, and although the day was a bright one it was dark inside, and spooky, and gutted of everything but the walls themselves. I tried to imagine her stopping at this gas station on her very first day here, nineteen years ago, pulling up to the pumps and waiting for some hayseed character in an oil-stained jumpsuit, wiping his hands on a dirty orange rag, shielding his eyes from the glare. Her hair would have been auburn, tied back in a scarf, her eyes green, her face lightly freckled. Her smile — her best quality, somebody told me — would have shined for the man. But the image quickly faded. I couldn't really fathom her then, make her real again in my mind.

But say she left the car as he was filling it and walked around the side of the station to the ladies' room. No door here either, just the toilet, the dim mirror, the sink. It was odd to think that her face might have been reflected here once, just as mine was now. If a mirror had a memory and could summon its stored images, I could have placed my face against hers and seen how one resembled the other, what matched and what didn't. Hair, mouth, eyes, chin. But even without this comparison I saw the resemblance: neither of us had a clue about what was about to happen.

"Hi, I'm Lucy Rider," she said to herself in the mirror. Or, working on that smile, lifting her shoulders: "Lucy Rider. Hello."

I looked at my own self. I said, "Hi, there. I'm Thomas." The mirror was so old now it barely maintained a reflection. It was not much better than a piece of tin, really, so I could hardly make myself out. White face, brown hair, green eyes. Lips, nose, and ears proportioned in a way that could be described only as normal. Of average height. An American, eighteen years of age, with a limp. As plain as the country air.

I walked around to the front of the gas station to the telephone booth there — the kind you don't see anymore — a glass rectangular box, like the one Superman used. The phone inside it actually worked. Rotary dial. I called Anna.

"Okay," I said. "Looks like I'm almost there."

"You're calling from the gas station?"

"From what's left of it," I said. "It's sort of out of business."

"Things change, huh?" she said. "In eighteen years."

And I thought about the road leading out to our farm, how it had been nothing but trees once, before so-called development, and how the opposite was happening here: the trees were coming back. I figured in a while there'd be nothing left to suggest a gas station had been here at all.

I said, "I guess I should head on into town."

"I guess you should," she said.

The town was just up the hill, but it looked far away now. Through the high weeds I could see what was left of an old sign, once painted bright red and green and black but now weathered and pale and leaning to one side. It said, WELCOME TO ASHLAND, WATERMELON CAPITAL OF THE WORLD!

"So," I said. "Tell me again?"

"Tell you what?"

"Why I'm doing this." My mouth was dry, and in my head I could hear my heart beating.

"Because it's what a man does," she said. "He goes on a journey."

"And why does he do that?"

"To find himself," she said.

"And I'm a man," I said.

"That's right," she said. "You're a man."

"And all those things you told me," I said. "About what happened to my mother there, in Ashland. They were true?"

"Yes," she said. "Crazy, but true. That was a long time ago though, Thomas. Things have changed. I'm sure."

"Sure," I said.

I felt like a detective brought on to a hopeless case eighteen years too late. This was the plan Anna and I had come up with: look around, talk to the people, ask a few questions. Excuse me, yes, good afternoon, are you familiar with the name Lucy Rider? Yes ma'am, that's right: Rider. It's known that she left the Birmingham area following the death of her mother, under the aegis of her father, who had "hired" her (a makeshift job, it appears, for a daughter who had few prospects) to check on several of the properties he owned throughout the state, and that in the course of her duties ended up staying on for a length of time here, in Ashland, where she eventually died. Yes ma'am: a good-looking woman, from what I hear. Thank you. Thank you very much. Oh. Another thing, ma'am. By the way: it's known as well that on the day she died she gave birth to a child, a son, named Thomas. Thomas Rider. He's the one I'm looking for, really. Yes ma'am.

If you see him, let me know.

The Story of the Watermelon King

They talked, I listened. I stood there, amazed. Everybody had a story, and they were all a little different, but this one was the same no matter who was telling it. It was the story of the Watermelon King, a story so old it came before the words were made to write it down. It came before the town and the men who built it, and the Indians who lived there before them. It was a story passed down through time by the sounds the most ancient man and woman made, and when they came here they learned to speak it too, and speak it now in their own voice, like this:

Once upon a long time ago, beneath this sun, in these fields, our world was full of watermelons. Everywhere you looked there were watermelons. You couldn't walk without stepping on them. No one person thought to grow them; they seemed to grow themselves. It was said you could watch a vine grow, that you could actually *see* it move, creeping along the ground as though groping for something to hold on to, that a watermelon would swell before your eyes like a balloon, and that some grew so large, so enormous, that children could stand upright within their hollowed-out shells.

During the peak of the season, when the air was hot and wet, people would wake after a night's sleep to find their homes encircled by vines, and more than one baby was known to be smothered as it lay on a blanket beside a particularly enterprising plot. Luckily, most people came to no harm. It was easy to cut the vines away from your house in the morning and pull them off as they coiled around your ankle.

Of course, this was in the before-times. Such legendary abundance did not last into the now. No one knows why this is so. But somewhere back within our dim history the watermelon became a thing to be planted and harvested, a crop like any other, sold to towns far and wide. In this way the Ashland watermelon, its great size and pleasing flavor, became well known throughout the world, and unmatched, and this small area of land was always considered blessed in some mysterious way by God, or by a god, our God. The watermelon was seen as a gift from this God, and to honor the watermelon was to honor God, and thus from the beginning, under the stewardship of men, there was a festival, an annual event, that occurred just before picking time.

During the festival the watermelon was celebrated in many ways. Songs were sung, and great murals drawn, and the man or woman who had grown the largest watermelon was brought before the town and revered.

But the amazing and unexplainable fertile nature of this town was the thing most celebrated. The soil and the sun were of course partners in the great mystery, and beyond our understanding. But there was no mystery about the first step: the seed of the watermelon must first be planted and grown. Fertility — that was everything. Without it, we were just another town.

And thus as the future of the town and the future of the watermelon seemed to be intertwined, in our minds the seed of the watermelon came to be understood as the same as the seed of a child, a boy who would grow into a farmer, a girl who would become a woman who would take care of a farmer, one neither more nor less than the other. These men and women would carry on after those who had tilled the soil so long before them had gone. For indeed, what does the burgeoning belly of a woman resemble as she becomes weighed down with the growing life inside her?

It was in this way that a male virgin was thought to bring a curse upon the town. If a man had reached manhood and was still a virgin, he was seen as a threat to the prosperity of the town, and thus each year one man was chosen to be cured. It was a sacrifice like all sacrifices. It was the sacrifice of his virginity.

This man came to be known through the agency of an old woman, a swamp dweller, who could look into a man's eyes and see, and with his body close, smell. A man who is still a virgin is not quite whole, and to look at him for a length of time is to see through him as though he were a pane of glass, and this woman could see such things.

The men of the village were thus inspected, and the oldest among them who had yet to be with a woman was chosen. He was brought before the town in a cart, as the sun set, at the very end of the festival. He would be the king. His crown, a hollowed-out rind; his scepter, a dried and withered vine. The people would watch, cheering him with their laughter. Then a ring of fire was set around him as the sun went down, and around this ring the town would slowly gather.

The man would stand within the circle, waiting, alone.

Then the three chosen women, dressed in simple, white cotton gowns, would steal away to a hut in the fields a distance away. In the center of the hut was a basket of watermelon seeds, cleaned and dried, hard and dark like small stones. But one seed was a seed of gold. Each woman reached into the basket and took a handful of seeds, and then the seeds were shown and the woman with the golden seed in her hand left the others and alone walked through the ring of fire. There she took the man's hand, and the two withdrew to a spot in the fields away from us all, and beneath the bright moon the man planted his seed within her; she would attest to it later in her own words, before us all. Thus the future of the town and the crop on which the town was founded was thought to be secure for yet another year, and from that day forward and throughout the year the man who had thus given himself to a woman for the first time was looked upon and acknowledged as the Watermelon King.

But if no virgin is sacrificed where a virgin be, then the gift we had been given would be taken away, and our crops would wither beneath the unforgiving sun, and we would be nothing.

Thus it is and thus it always was, even before the words were made to write it down.

Old Man

A broken and wrinkled man, blind in one milky-white eye, sits on a bench beneath an awning in front of the hardware store. One hundred years old if he is a day. I smile, wave, and he does the same. Talk to anybody, *Anna said.* Talk to everybody. One thing about those people, *she said,* they love to talk.

Ashland, Alabama, our little town, was founded in the late-eighteenth century by people of German descent, though I suspect most of whatever that strain entailed has been bred out over time. Not too many Germans here that *I* know of. Hard work is something we have always believed in, though, and maybe that's German, I don't know. But then, hard work is about all that has ever been offered. Imagine how arduous it was to construct this place, to get through the rocks, through the trees, up the slant of every hill. There is no flat place in the foothills, no solid ground. No spot not made craggy and pitted by time. And yet someone thought this was a good place for a town. I blame the Germans.

We're *stoics.* We're the kind of folk who celebrate the living, bury the dead, and move on. That's us. When it rains, it doesn't surprise us at all. We expect it, and we get out our umbrellas. Other people — "Too wet to plow, too dry to plow, too hot to plow, too cold to plow" — that's not us, never has been. Not so much plowing done these days, of course. Now it's mostly service industries for work, and the various plants in the county, such as your towel- and rug-manufacturing concerns. It's still work, though, and it's hard. Some of us barely get by.

We base our lives on the word of God. We're mostly Baptist, but there are Presbyterians and Episcopalians and your rock-bed fundamentalists. A few snake charmers. No Catholics or Jews that I know of, not a one. But there are more churches here than there are bars, and that counts for something. A *lot* of praying goes on. It's like a hobby. I don't see that it does all that much good, though, to be honest. Why would a just God put a plague on our fields? But we still go to church, every Sunday. Town shuts down on a Sunday, but for the Steak and Egg and the fast-food joints by the highway.

I guess it would come as no surprise to discover that we're quite conservative. Most normal, average people here are so far right that it doesn't take much deviation further in the same direction to become a fanatic. So we do have a few maniacs running around.

Having a lot of black people around is *not* our idea of a good time. But then I reckon there are a lot of black people who would say the same about us. Of course, you can't talk about that.

I remember a story from a few years back. One of our boys risked his own life to save a black child in the river. It was the day after a big rain and the current was strong, scary. He dove in, nearly drowning himself, but was able to drag the boy to the bank. Asked why he did such a foolish, heroic thing, all he said was "Boy couldn't swim." Human beings are complex.

We tell a lot of stories. I may be lying to you now — who's to say? It's just part of who we are. Nothing is as big or as loud or as blue or as soft as we say it is — and not because real life is a plain thing but because adding to the common stock of experience through confabulation seems to be a human job, one we're definitely up to. The truth is like a fish, isn't it? Nearly impossible to grab hold of. So we don't put much stead in it and have fun watching the fools who do, splashing away.

So, that's turn-of-the-century Ashland for you. A few thousand people live here. Some come, some go, some come and go. If there's a deep kinship among us, it's because so many of us are kin. There's really no limit to the number of branches on our family trees. I think I'm related to my wife in some distant way, and somehow that's reassuring to me. Anyway, what real choice do we have? Ashland is not a place that many people yearn to come to, especially since — no more watermelon.

I tell you, though, when new people do come here and stay, it is something! It's as though our lives are lived through an eternal dark night, and then someone new comes around, and it's like looking to the sky, where all of a sudden there's this *bright light,* like the tail of a comet, and as it gets closer and closer you realize it's coming down somewhere close, close, *oh my gosh it's coming down right in your own backyard!* And the impact makes everything shake and everyone shudder. There's no one who can say they're not changed by such an event. No one.

So sure, to answer your question — I remember your mother. I remember her driving into town, red hair back in a scarf, wind blowing through the open window, parking in the spot right over there and getting out, taking a look at the place. I remember her coming and everything that happened after.

I even remember you.

Mrs. Parsons, Innkeeper

Another small wrinkled person, and her house had that old person's smell. When I told her my name, she seemed dazed for a moment, and then looked at me, wide-eyed, as if she had a clearer idea of who I was than I did. But she was sweet and friendly. When she talked, little flecks of white collected in the corners of her mouth. The old man had told me where she lived because she rented out the second story of the white brick house she lived in to people passing through and I needed a place to stay.

I was thinking about your mother, Lucy Rider, just last week. Not *thinking* about her, really. But her name just popped into my head, even though it's been so many years. I've got a black girl working for me now, and her name is Lucy, and sometimes saying her name, calling out for her, makes me think *Lucy Rider.* I wondered if something happened to her, then I remembered: of course. She's dead. She's dead and yet I wouldn't be surprised if something was happening with her still, even now, in the other world. I think your mother must be popular there as well. Something was *always* happening with her. There are those rare people who function like *human magnets,* who are individually so attractive — or repellent, depending on the situation — that a considerable amount *more* seems to happen to them, and, likewise, their presence in a certain place makes *more* seem to happen around them. They're magical people. They have a special power.

This is how I saw your mother.

My husband — he died seven years ago this spring — was just the opposite. He was a neutral force. He moved through the world like an invisible man. Now, we had a good life. He sold office supplies, which meant he had to travel a good bit in the beginning. But not a thing ever happened to him. Not one accident, *ever.* By his last few years he had established a number of solid accounts and merely had to resupply them by phone. Sometimes I could just watch him at the kitchen table, filling out order sheets, sipping from a glass of tea, dressed in one of his suits as though he were going to an office somewhere. We had two daughters, both married now and moved away, and they have inherited his gift for invisibility. Nothing ever happens to them. It's as if their lives are being lived in the *margins,* on the outer edge of a *forest;* they're not really living so much as simply *being alive,* a condition that neither surprises nor delights them. It's probably *best* to be invisible, everything being equal. It's not always a positive, to be large, to glow, to attract the world, moth to flame. Like your mother.

I miss my husband. There's a hole in the world now, this empty space his life used to fill. I mean that in the most literal way. I pass through these pockets of cold air, even on the warmest day, and I know these are places he was meant to inhabit. His name was Thomas too, you know. Tom, I called him. Old Tom. A good name.

So, I have to ask myself, and you have to ask yourself, why did I think of Lucy Rider last week? A coincidence? That's a cause for laughter there, isn't it? The fact that I hadn't thought of her in some years, and then I did, and then, here you are, and that's a *coincidence?* We could laugh about that all week. Could your plans to come here in some way have caused the thought? Did your plan directly *coincide* with my thought? All I know is that I spend a good part of my day sifting through my brain like it's a box of old photographs, and last week I came upon one of your mother.

She took a good picture, I bet.

I won't say I knew her very well. We met on several occasions, but we never — not that she wasn't friendly. She was a very active, energetic young woman, involved in the life — and death — of Ashland in so many different ways. Because of her we no longer have a Watermelon Festival. It was like Christmas, the festival, but just for us, for Ashland. Imagine not having Christmas anymore. That's what it's like now, because of her. But then it was terrible — terrible, what happened to her. I look back on that time with great regret. I should have *done* more, should have reached out to her, in some way. But at that time in my life I didn't want to be close to a woman like her. I was more comfortable with my invisible husband and children. If she were to come back now, though, I think I'd be knocking on her door. I'd be her best friend. I've opened myself up to things since then. That comes from being alone.

Terry Smith, Realtor

My grandfather was a realtor, so when I saw the sign it felt like home, and I walked right in. Terry Smith worked in a small office on the corner of Fourth Street and Main. Her desk was crowded with gold-framed pictures of her family, and this made me think about how much I would like to be able to do that — have a picture, like this, of my family. She acted and dressed more like a beauty queen than a woman who had to be in her late fifties. The pants suit she wore was a bright orange color and so tight it embarrassed me, and her hair was short and modern, dyed a chestnut brown. She was perky; if I hadn't been there, I had the feeling she'd be talking to my empty chair.

I have an incredible memory. No brag, just fact. When I was a kid I about *memorized* the *Guinness Book of World Records.* Who was the tallest man in the world? Robert Wadlow, eight eleven. The shortest? Gul Mohammed, twenty-two inches. That's less than two feet tall. He lived in India. See? The most seeds ever found in a watermelon? One thousand, one hundred and twenty-two. I could go on. My husband says I'm an idiot savant — with emphasis on the idiot part! — but men like to make fun of a woman's skills, don't they? It's how they feel better about themselves.

So, sure. I can tell you a thing or two about Lucille Rider. That's what I called her. *Lucille.* What a pretty name. It was nineteen, nineteen . . . nineteen eighty-two. The spring. She sat in the very same chair you're sitting in now (those chairs are built to last) and we talked about this and that. The skirt she was wearing *was* a tad short for Ashland, or maybe her legs were a tad long, and I thought, *Dear God, sweetheart, leave* something *to the imagination,* but I kept my own counsel. Judge not lest ye be judged, I said, not that I've been spared the judgment, the pettiness, and the rampant small-mindedness this town specializes in. When I was a cheerleader in high school I fell from the top of a human pyramid at halftime. I wasn't physically hurt — Todd Eakins almost caught me, and helped break the fall — but I can't trip over a crack in the sidewalk today without someone saying, "There she goes again." Or thinking it. *Is there nothing more pleasurable to one human being than the failure of another?* I've yet to find out. When I fell off that pyramid people gathered around me all concerned, but you could see it in their eyes, what they were thinking: *You're not so high and mighty now, Miss Cheerleader.* It's a look your mother saw too, I imagine, toward the end. After everything she had done to us. She was like me like that. The higher you go, the longer the fall. And she fell. But that's not what I wanted to tell you about.

Your mother needed my help finding a house she said belonged to her father. Told me she was checking up on his *various properties.* That's how she said it — "various properties," which made him seem like a trillionaire and her like a trillionaire's daughter. She had a sheet of paper with addresses on it. The one she was trying to read for me, the location was all marked with a pen, so she had trouble reading it. But then she sussed it out and read it to me, the address, and I looked at it twice and then I looked at her and said, "Are you *sure* this is the right address?" She was sure. She asked me, "Do you know the house?"

I said, "Lord, woman. Do I ever. Why is it all marked up, though?"

"Oh," she said. "He told me it wasn't necessary that I check on this one. But I've done all the others. And I don't want to go home."

"Looking for a little excitement, are you?" I said.

"Something," she said. "Anything but going home."

"Well, let's go check it out!"

A nice-looking young woman, your mother. She had a glaze on her, a *patina,* that had not been scratched by anything. She indicated that this was her first job, she had just left home, and so I imagined the hard times for her were just beginning.

Anyway, we took a little ride around town in my car so she could have a look-see before we got to her father's place. It was raining and the sun was shining at the same time, the way it does sometimes, and I said, "Somewhere, a monkey's laughing." And she looked at me, real surprised. "My daddy says that," she said. "I never heard anybody say that before but him." "I reckon a lot of people say it," I said, and she said she reckoned they did too. After that she sat real quiet on her side of the car, a perfect little lady. Ten minutes of driving around, though, and she starts getting all fidgety and says, "Do you mind if I smoke?" I said no and she lit up right quick, blowing the smoke through those lips like a chimney and coughing.

"I just started," she said. She laughed and looked out the window. "My mother died six weeks ago, and for some reason, right after that happened, I thought smoking looked like something I could do. I felt like it might help me in some way. I guess that's crazy."

"Not at all," I said. "Sorry about your mother. What took her?"

"Cancer," she said. "Cancer of the brain." She looked out the window again. "I just get an *empty* feeling inside of me," she said. "Do you know what I mean?"

"I do," I said. "Time. Just give it time." Because what else am I going to say? I hardly knew the woman and here she was telling me about her dead mother.

Finally, we were coasting down Ninth Street and came to the dead end, and I backed out and turned around and said, "Well, there she is."

We took a moment to stare — she, a little stunned. Because who wouldn't be?

It was the old Hargraves place. Empty for about six years by then, and it looked it. Shingles all over the yard, paint peeling, ivy about to overtake it with a vengeance. The Hargraveses themselves had been dead for a long time, and other people had lived there on and off since, renters, all of them, but it was still known as the Hargraves place, and it still is today. I heard her gulp a helping of air. None of the other "properties" she was viewing looked quite like this, I gathered. She touched a charm bracelet she was wearing on her wrist, just touched it with her fingers. There was like a little heart I think, and a house, maybe a key, and some other things, all pretty and dangling. I remember because they all seemed to mean something. To her, anyway. You could just tell. Then she sighed and said, "Well, let's take a look around."

We did, and it was an absolute wreck. The ceilings were sagging in places, the wallpaper peeling, and there was this awful mildew smell. Some of the windows had been knocked out so there were nests inside — squirrel nests, I imagine. But it didn't seem to bother her. She had this *look* in her eyes for some reason — they were just shining. She touched the dusty banister, looked up, and smiled. The first time I'd seen her really smile.

"Good for sliding down," she said, "if you were a child."

"If you were a child that liked splinters," I said.

Well, it just got worse and worse, from the kitchen to the basement to the bedrooms upstairs. There were actual *bats* in the attic. Actual bats! But again, you know, in my business it pays to keep an open mind, because one man's dump is another man's castle. Or woman's, in this case.

"This place is going to need some work," she said to me, nodding. "I might be here for some time," she said.

What happened next was kind of strange. She turned to me and said, "Mrs. Smith, is there anything you can tell me about the people who lived here before? The Hargraveses? Because I'm getting this feeling," she said. "What kind of feeling would *that* be?" I said. But she couldn't put her finger on it. She touched her charm bracelet instead. "Something . . . *familiar*," she said, in a dreamy sort of way.

A nice girl, your mother. It's hard to think of her the way people'd like you to, even after all that happened. Because she wasn't evil. I really don't think she was evil at all. That's what a woman becomes, though, to a man anyway, when she uses her sex to her own advantage. And Lucille did. Not with Iggy Winslow, of course. But with Carlton Snipes, and Sugar and the rest. She used her sex and she got what she wanted, and sometimes that's the only thing a woman can do.

On the other hand, maybe it had something to do with the house.

Old Man

This is the Hargraves story.

Justin Hargraves was a man so full of hate that it made his blood run thin and cold, so his skin was always a deathly white, and his eyes no more than thin dark slits cut into his face. When he smiled you knew some evil thought was swimming around his brain, an idea of some minor harm he could cause another, and when he was happy you knew he had already caused it. Somehow he had a wife. Over the years he had drained the life out of her, and then, when they had a son, people expected the same would happen to him. But this is not what happened.

Hargraves was equally unkind to everybody, but he held a special hatred in his heart for the Negroes. He was not alone, of course. Many of us hated and feared them. But his voice could be heard above the rest. He posted a sign one day that read NIGGER, DON'T LET THE ASHLAND SUN SET ON YOUR BACK. And no one took it down. At that time, the train tracks marked the city's limit. The Negroes lived on the other side of it, but they could see his sign from their houses.

Hargraves ran a fertilizer business. Sometimes the Negroes would complain, quietly, that the bags they bought from him contained mostly sand. No one doubted this was true, because Hargraves was so happy to sell to them. Years and years went by, and nothing changed.

But during these years Hargraves's son grew into a man, and

as he did the town looked on in wonder, because soon it became clear that some cosmic mistake had been made. This boy was not his father's son. He was smart, good-hearted, and his every thought and deed seemed designed to benefit another. When he was sixteen he began to work with his father at the fertilizer company, and soon thereafter the Negroes began to notice the absence of sand in their bags. Complicit in his goodness, they said nothing.

Hargraves didn't know what to make of his child. He felt as though he had been cursed in some way. He stayed away from his son for the most part, and his son from him, because when they faced each other the air seemed to disappear from a room. Hargraves told stories about his son to others, stories that made him seem weak and traitorous. And his son *was* traitorous — to him, to what he stood for in this town and in the world.

What happened next was beyond anything anyone could have imagined. When the boy was seventeen, he was taller than his father, and proud of his goodness. One night father and son stayed in the same room too long. They fought. Not with their fists, though it almost came to that. In the end the son ran from the house and got in his car, as if by doing this he could somehow escape. In his righteous, youthful anger he drove through town fast, too fast. But he knew where he was going. He was on his way to the tracks. He was going to rip down that sign his father had painted and posted a dozen years before. When he was almost there a dog appeared briefly in his headlights, so suddenly he didn't have time to stop his car. And it was close, but the dog passed safely into the surrounding darkness like a shadow, and the boy, his heart racing, slowed down. But not enough. He didn't see the man until he was just upon him, until like some ghostly apparition he sprang up fully formed, huge-seeming, and terrifying, in the light. He saw the man's face, and caught the recognition of fate in his eyes, before the car knocked the man flat over, felling him like a tree. It was a Negro — Sam Boudreaux. The boy had sold fertilizer to him time and again. He knew his face. He knew his family. It would later be revealed that normally Sam wouldn't have been out so late, on the other side of the tracks. But he'd been after his dog, who had jumped his pen into the dangerous Ashland night.

Hargraves, when he learned of it later that evening, found the irony of his son's situation beautiful. Certainly, he had often entertained notions of killing a Negro, and, when he was a boy, had even seen one killed, hung from a tree like a Halloween ornament, but that was an even longer time ago, when justice was impossible for some and expedient for others. So perhaps he was even a little envious of his son. Hargraves, being Hargraves, could never have gotten away with it. Only his son, in his pure and awful goodness, could do what he had done and not have to pay for it. Hargraves knew he would not have to pay.

The boy, of course, was desolate. His spirit crumbled. His eyes, once so bright, became bleak and vacant. It was an accident, and yet the fact that it was an accident changed nothing. A man was dead. He turned himself in to the sheriff that night. The sheriff listened to his story, and then told him to go home, and as if that were a final, inviolable order, that is what he did, and nothing else. He went to his room and stayed there, without eating, for days. It was as though he had sentenced himself to his own prison and would serve out his sentence there.

Hargraves knew the sheriff well. Ashland was a smaller town back then. They drank coffee together in the morning, before heading off to work, in the café downtown. The morning after the accident the sheriff spoke with him about his boy. It was a difficult situation, they both agreed. Things get difficult when there's a body at the morgue and a family grieving, no matter who that family is.

No matter who, Hargraves said.

That's right.

You can't just, you know, ignore it. Not anymore. Much as you'd like to.

There's has to be some recompense, the sheriff said. *Something to satisfy those people. Any little thing like this can give them a reason to set off. It's different now. They've got a voice.*

And so it was decided that Hargraves's boy would have to leave town. If he didn't, no one could say what might happen.

At first the boy refused. He wanted to face the consequences of his actions. He wanted to pay. That was the only way he would be able to go on with his life. He went down to the jail and told the sheriff this, and the sheriff, in his wisdom, took him back to an empty cell and beat him with his hands to within an inch of his life. Nearly killed him. *A preview of coming attractions,* the sheriff said. *Every day for the rest of your fucking life unless you make the right decision.* He spoke to the bloody body, eyes staring up at him as if from the edge of death itself. *Forget what happened,* he said. *Forget Ashland. Forget the nigger, forget your father, forget everything. This is nothing to you now. Nothing. Leave here tonight or I can't help you.*

And in the morning, the boy had gone. The sheriff told the family of the dead man that the police would do everything they could to find him and bring him to justice, but everybody knew this was a lie. They knew he would be gone for three, four years, until things had cooled down, the event forgotten, or at worst a distant memory. And then one day he would reappear and assume his place in the life of Ashland. This was the plan — unspoken, but the plan, nonetheless. After it all blew over — this is what Hargraves told everybody — after it all blew over, his son — a killer now, a murderer, an accomplished boy — would come back, move right back into the house with his folks, and take over the fertilizer business. Then he would be coming here to the café downtown with the rest of them, a cup of coffee every morning. And a day didn't go by when Hargraves didn't tell somebody how it was going to be, as if by voicing it he could somehow make it happen, that he could make his son come back. Because Hargraves found that he actually missed his son. He didn't know why. He had never felt love for him — he didn't know if he had ever felt love for anything in his life — but now with his son gone there was a depth of emptiness inside that he never had known before, as if a part of him were missing. Even when his wife died, just a year after these events, Hargraves didn't feel the same pain he did in his son's absence. The only thing that made him feel better was when he would imagine the day the boy would return, and talk about it in the morning, drinking coffee with his friends.

But it didn't happen. The boy never came back. Hargraves died here, in his living room, his chair turned to face the window, waiting for his son. Sometimes people passing by say they can see his ghost, his face at the window, staring out into the distance, still waiting.

Carlton Snipes, Watermelon Festival Committee Chairman

It didn't take long, after I arrived in Ashland, for me to stop looking for people to talk to about my mother: they found me. It was as if they had been waiting. Carlton Snipes was one of the first to seek me out. A stern, serious, and completely bald man, Snipes looked like he was made out of wood. He sat upright, petrified, behind a large wooden desk in his home office. Degrees from two state universities were framed and hung on the wall behind him. He rocked back and forth in his creaky chair as we talked, his fingertips pressed together in an inverted V. He didn't blink.

I hate to be the one to say it, Mr. Rider, but when a woman opens her legs for a man only one good thing can happen. Everything else — well, it's in the eye of the beholder. I see I'm embarrassing you. You're a young man, unacquainted with these things. Am I right? I'm sorry. But it's the act of sex that made it so we were able to survive, and an act of sex, finally, that killed us. Perhaps we should talk about other, less challenging, topics.

The festival. Yes. I don't think we can underestimate what the Watermelon Festival meant to this town. Even to those who professed a studied *disinterest* in the whole affair, who displayed a kind of *cavalier remoteness* when the subject arose, be it on a street corner or in a classroom or at the Steak and Egg, over coffee, the

Watermelon Festival remained even in their lives a touchstone event.

It is, Mr. Rider, the glue that held us all together.

How can I say this without laughing, or provoking laughter from a young man such as yourself?

Two things, Mr. Rider.

Listen well.

One: the Watermelon Festival was our heritage. Heritage — it's just a word to you, no doubt. But in fact, heritage is something possessed as a result of one's *natural situation* — look it up. It's a birthright, a way of seeing and understanding who you are. This is something you should understand better than most, since, I imagine, that's why you're here yourself — to discover whatever heritage it is you have. Of course, I wish you all the luck in the world.

As for us, though, the people of Ashland, we know what our heritage was. And it's gone. Excuse me if I become nostalgic. But we'd had a Watermelon Festival as long as anyone could remember. It was both the economic and spiritual engine of our town. Alas, we no longer have enough watermelons to become festive over. Oh, yes, there's a patch here and there, and we have a small celebration, a remnant of times past, but we are no longer the so-called Watermelon Capital of the World and haven't been for years. The jury is still out on why this happened. Perhaps it was faulty crop rotation. Perhaps we didn't let the fields lie fallow for the appropriate length of time. Perhaps, finally, it was downy mildew and bacterial wilt. Or — as long as we're hypothesizing — maybe it had something to do with your mother. This may be what I believe. But none of this matters now. The fact is, up until the time your mother came to Ashland we had a festival, we had watermelons, and after her, we didn't. People used to come here from as far away as Kansas, one man all the way from *Japan,* to see this town. *That's* a heritage. Now the majority of the watermelons you see and even eat while you're here are brought in from other towns. Other towns that also grow tomatoes and squash. But we — Ashlanders — we look at the watermelons and in them we see who we *are*, because in them we see who we *were*.

Two: when your mother put an end to the festival, there was a huge uproar in this town the likes of which I haven't seen, oh, since the Hargraves incident some years back. Even though Miss Rider was well liked for the most part (though I would not necessarily say respected), to have her — a veritable stranger — object to our heritage (and what is heritage but the historical reflection of a people's soul?) — the ending, how it would all transpire, well, it was tragic. What happened to her. And yet how could it have happened otherwise? After all, we welcomed her with open arms, and she repaid us by attempting to destroy our entire town. And with Iggy Winslow, of all people.

Granted, the Watermelon King aspect of the festival may be seen as tasteless and offensive. It's irresponsible to actually promote sex in this day and age. But let's be frank: people around here are more concerned about the seed count of the biggest watermelon in town than they are about something like AIDS or what have you. This is something that you, being an outsider, cannot understand. It's our *history*. So I supported the festival in its every aspect, and I would again. It was our prosperity. The streets were cleaner then, people were happier, even the sun seemed to shine a little bit brighter. The Watermelon King is symbolic of all we once had and have now lost. And we cling to it still, because if we lose that, that memory, then what do we have? Nothing. We're nothing but another town.

That's what your mother wanted to turn us into. Just another town. Another dot on the map. Whether she knew it or not, this is what she wanted. And this is what we have almost become. Once my generation goes, no one will know that this was once a very special place. That for a few days every year, every man, woman, and child shared between them this single idea, and celebrated it, and were made better by it in every imaginable way. It's sad, to me, that those days are gone. I am an old man who lives in the past. And you are a young one.

Welcome to Ashland, Mr. Rider. I knew you would return.

Jonah Carpenter, Carpenter

Jonah Carpenter was a short, wiry man who, on the morning we met, and probably the morning before that, didn't shave. Whiskers stuck out of his chin like iron filings. His eyes were dim and kind, but really bloodshot. This, in addition to his complexion and the way his gnarled, spotted hands shook when he tried to rest them on his desk, made me think he had a drinking problem. When he coughed something always came up, and he gently removed whatever it was with a handkerchief, briefly taking a look at it. He'd come over to Mrs. Parsons's to fix a hole in the attic where the squirrels got in, and I talked to him while he worked.

In the beginning, when all the naming of things not named was being done, people were called what they were. Every town had a miller and a smithy and a farmer and a carpenter and whatnot, and so that's what they got to be called: Mr. Smith, Mr. Miller, Mr. Farmer. Over time, of course, like everything else, the tradition got muddled. Now you've got your names that don't mean anything at all! You have your Mr. Newby, your Mr. Edmunds. I'm against it.

So I'm a carpenter. My father was a carpenter and his father before him, on back to the beginning I reckon. My son doesn't much like carpentry, but what can I tell him? It's his destiny. I told him, Your name is not Jimmy Sleep-Late-in-the-Morning. Your name is not Jimmy Easy-Money. Your name is Jimmy Carpenter. You're a Carpenter. Get used to it.

When I first met your mother and she told me her name I looked her in the eye and said, "Rider. Lucy Rider. Historically, I imagine your folks rode horses or some such. Is that true?"

She said, "I don't know."

I said, "Horses, I bet, hundreds of years ago."

And she said, "Well, I'm riding a Cougar now."

And she winked at me and laughed. I laughed too. Because she was meaning her car. I saw it there in the drive.

Your mother was a pure sweetheart and a pleasure to view from every angle. That being said, as a businessman, I saw the Hargraves place and what had to be done, and little dollar signs were everywhere. I could tell in a flash that this was going to get into the hundreds of dollars. I gave her the estimate, wrote it out on a sheet of paper, and she didn't even look at it.

"Mr. Carpenter," she said. "I should tell you. I don't have much money."

I said, "Well, that could be a problem."

She said, "I wasn't expecting such a big job. I mean, I'm on a budget."

"What about your father?" I said. "It's his house, right?"

"I was hoping I could do this," she said. "This whole job — going around, checking on his properties — he just made it up to give me something to do. But I want to show him I can do something, really *do* something, on my own."

"That's admirable," I said. "But what about me?"

"Well, I was hoping we could barter our services."

"Barter," I said. "What do you mean, 'barter'?"

I knew the word but I didn't know how she meant it in this context, you know.

"Well," she said. "Before there was money, people used to exchange skills. A person who made bread, for instance —"

"Mr. Baker," I said.

"— might trade that bread for seeds to grow plants."

"Mr. Melon."

"Exactly. I was hoping we could do the same thing."

I nodded, taking it all in. This spoke to me, of course, and somehow she knew it would. I was ready to trade.

"I make," she said, "the best lunch in Alabama."

"You do, do you?" I said, narrowing my eyes to mask my disappointment.

"The best. I used to make them for my father, who wouldn't have eaten at all had I not made the most remarkable and amazing sandwiches ever and brought them to his desk. He's a realtor, Mr. Carpenter. But he's also quite a reader. A man lost in a world of ideas."

"A bookworm," I said.

"Exactly. But my sandwiches brought him back to this world. Egg salad, tuna salad, hamburger, grilled cheese, even peanut butter and jelly. One bite, just one, and the taste of it brought him back from whatever distant place his mind had roamed, and he would look at me as if he had suddenly snapped out of a trance and say, *You have outdone yourself today, Lucy,* or, *This is a culinary miracle,* or *As ambrosia is on Mount Olympus, so this sandwich is to me.*"

"I love peanut butter and jelly," I said.

"I make them," she said, "with the jelly on top. That makes all the difference."

And I could imagine how that would.

"So, my proposition is: I'll make you lunch every day until my bill is paid, each lunch constituting a portion of the fee, or until that time when I have the money to pay you back properly."

So. I'm going to say no to that? I don't think so. It turned out to be a real good deal for me, though. What she said about her sandwiches was true. Best I ever had. Even after I finished the job and moved on to another, there'd be a bag lunch waiting for me at my desk every morning, or sitting in the cab of my truck. I began to count on it. It was something different every day. Turkey, roast beef, BLT. And, of course, the peanut butter and jelly, with the jelly on top. I'd call her up to thank her. We kept in touch. She settled into the life of the town real nice. Made some friends. Started doing that work with Iggy. And then the festival, of course. But before all that happened, I'd call her up and say, "That was a real nice sandwich, Lucy," or, "That really hit the spot, what you made today," or I'd say, you know, because I knew she wanted to hear it, she wanted to hear it more than anything else, "Ambrosia, Lucy," I'd tell her. "Really. Ambrosia."

Iggy Winslow, Idiot

Though he turned out to be a friendly person, Iggy scared me at first. I won't describe him, because he described himself pretty well in his own words, but there was something frightening about the way he was: not really a man, not really a boy, full of thoughts beyond his ability to express them. It turned out we had many things in common, including a limp.

I swear to God if there is a God, and if not, I just swear. It's a relief to me either way. I keep trying to figure out what the big difference would be. But it all comes down to having somebody to blame, I guess. I can blame God or I can blame my mom and dad for making me who I am and then dying, or just whoever's handy. Sugar, the old people, this town. But here I am, still Iggy. I just feel like *someone* should take responsibility for this . . . what do you call it . . . defective workmanship. Someone should take the blame, get fired or . . . I don't know. Because there is something *wrong* with the way I was made. First, you know, I look like something that got put together from *the parts of other people*. I look at myself in the mirror and just wonder at how it all sticks together. And sometimes I think only God could have made something as weird as me and other times, other times I think no god could have let anything like this happen. Either way, here I am, still Iggy. Amount of change: none.

I met your mom because I mowed her lawn. She came out while I was mowing it, and said, "Excuse me, but what are you doing?" And I said, "Me? I am mowing your lawn." I forgot she was new. I thought somebody might have told her I mowed the lawns around here. In Ashland that's what happens. I see a lawn that needs mowing and I mow it. It's a full-time job. There's a jar behind the counter at the Steak and Egg where people used to leave some money, like a collection. When I needed cash I'd just get it from the jar. It was a nice little system created in compensation for my extreme fucked-up-ness, and I appreciated it.

But your mom didn't know about it, and she wondered what I was doing out there and I had to tell her — kind of nervous and stuttering and all because no one had ever asked me before what I was doing, and she was so beautiful — I tried to say what it was I was doing. She got it eventually, nodding, all patient the way she was. Then she walked me out to a patch of clover to one side of her mailbox, just this patch of plain old clover, and she asked if I would spare her that, because it was pretty and she liked to look at it, and I said I would, and I did.

Something about that moment we shared, though, standing above the clover, that plus the fact that she was as pretty as anything I had ever seen in my life before, made me want to know her forever. And more, if I could. Not that I could. All I knew is, I just couldn't wait for her grass to grow so I could come back.

She wore the prettiest sundresses, white and yellow and covered with blue and purple flowers. All wavy and loose. Sometimes she'd wear her hair up, to give her neck some air she said, and she looked nice that way. But then when she'd take it down, the way it tumbled off her head and rolled across her shoulders in waves, and colored like fire, the way fire is not just one color but about seven, all becoming one another over and back again: that was her hair. The green eyes, the smile, and then — well, pardon me if I mention this — her whole body. I cannot lie about that. In this world though, people are made to want the thing that is most impossible to have. Did you know that? That's my theory. And I have always wanted to be close to a woman. It was always my big dream. When I was boy and I slept with my dog, JoJo — he was a kind of German shepherd/pointer thing — I held him in my arms at night like another person, and he stretched out long against me and we spooned, and it was *so warm,* especially in February, when it gets so cold around here. I pretended with him — just sleeping, and holding him, in my mind.

He died when I was seventeen, just before your mom came here. Run over. Sugar did it. Accident, he said.

I never forgave him, though. I just can't.

So. I guess I was on the rebound from that when I met Lucy, but then my heart has always been a wide-open thing.

Al Speegle, Pharmacist

Al Speegle moved slowly, as though each step were mapped out in advance but he was having trouble remembering the directions. Though in his late sixties, he had a head full of youngish brown hair and the handsome, ageless face of a TV actor. His teeth were large and white, his shoulders broad, his demeanor reassuring. I liked him.

The history of "pharmacy" and the whole pharmacological tradition is actually quite interesting, so before we talk about your mother I'd like to say a few words about it, since you're already here and it's not often that I get to talk about these things, my children having left the nest and having a wife whose interests are limited to the eradication of dust and the growing of the perfect tomato. It's a fascinating subject, especially considering the dim light in which most people hold pharmacists. It's amazing how many people think of us as *failed doctors*. Or as failures, pure and simple. But how many people know that since the beginning of recorded time the art of healing has always recognized a separation between the duties of the physician and those of the herbalist, who supplied the physician with the raw materials to make medicine? Blessed few. The physician-priests of Egypt were divided into two classes: those who visited the sick and those who remained in the temple and prepared remedies for the sick. One finds it difficult to imagine an Egyptian priest being treated — or even thought of — the way his professional descendants are today. And in China, *please.* Without the pharmacist there's no Eastern medicine. Period. But after World War Two, especially in this country, the pharmacist's stock plummeted. Benjamin Franklin — the father of pharmacy in America — is turning *in his grave.* Did you know we pharmacists used to actually *make* pills? True. Plasters, potions, cachets. Not anymore, of course. We're basically a dispensary. But the profession has a noble heritage and that counts for something, I think. I know quite a bit about most people. A pharmacist knows a great deal more than people give him credit for: secrets, large and small. The medication we take to keep us normal, or to make us better than normal, these things I know. In many ways, a pharmacist is a modern variant on the ancient village wise man. That's why I'm slightly elevated. At the pharmacy. I look down on everybody. Or, rather, people look up to me.

Not that I ever wanted to be a pharmacist. From the time I was little, I have always wanted to be a commercial pilot. I was a child, of course, and children long to be such things. But I have never stopped wanting to fly the big planes. Ever. My room was plastered with posters of DC-9s and such. And the models I built! It was a lifelong dream. Eventually my mother dissuaded me. She simply forbade it. It wasn't sensible, she said. She said I should become a pharmacist, of all things! And I did. Why couldn't she have just let me do what I wanted? *Where's the harm in that?* I've never forgiven her for this, or myself for not following my dream. Though I couldn't generalize this rule to everybody. No. I would still have to say to children everywhere: *listen to your mother.*

Lucy Rider.

It was almost tragic, in my opinion, how beautiful she was. By tragic I mean that she looked like some kind of movie star, with a face of such perfection and radiance that having looked at it once you found that falling in love with her was not merely a possibility, but a duty. A duty of the heart. But her beauty was wasted here, in this little town. That was the tragedy. It would be equally tragic, for instance, to have, oh, *Einstein* working as an accountant, or Bach writing jingles for soft drink advertisements. Her beauty, I mean, was a kind of genius, big enough for the whole world. She had light brown hair that, in a certain light, turned red. Or red hair that in a certain light turned brown. I'm not sure now. It waved and curled to her shoulders. Green eyes, white, freckled skin. And when she came in to pick up a prescription and said my name, it was as though no one had ever said it before. *Mr. Speegle.* The way she said it, I mean. It was how my name was supposed to sound. No one else ever . . . got it quite right.

So, yes, I fell in love with her, and I can name fifty other men who fell in love with her as well, in love with the *life* in her, or the way, when she was thinking, she touched her charm bracelet ever so lightly. It amazed me — amazed us all, I think — how quickly she became a part of this town. A necessary part. And a part we didn't even know was missing, until she showed us. In a matter of weeks she walked these streets as though she had been here forever — shopping, making friends, and, like you, asking questions. Beauty is a ticket to the world. Not that there was anything to be done about it from my end. I was married. I should say I was happily married. *Am* happily married. I had no intention, of course, of leaving my wife for your mother. The thought never crossed my mind. But there would be those times when my mind would drift, and my eyes would get that blank look in them, and my wife would ask me, "What are you thinking about?" And I would say, "Oh, nothing." I would be thinking about your mother.

She was a pleasant thought. It was not, as you might think, a fantasy. I didn't fantasize about your mother. I just thought of her the way she was. Harmless thoughts — as I looked up from my perch at the back of the store at the precise moment she appeared before the glass doors, for instance, which meant I was going to get to see her walk all the way across the store. This was a treat. Maybe she'd be wearing the cotton dress with the spring floral pattern and a light blue sweater. Or the black turtleneck and that red skirt. But when I caught her at that moment, just entering, I could watch her glide down the aisles, across the chipped and scarred linoleum, picking up toothpaste, floss, some lady things, until finally she would arrive at her destination — me. This is the sort of thing I would think about. And the odd thing was, I knew I was not the only one. At that very moment, there were other men — and women too, I imagine: why not? — who were also thinking about your mother. Where was the harm in thinking about her? It would have been more tragic had we disallowed ourselves even that. In my opinion.

My wife will be home soon. Perhaps we should finish up. Not that we can't talk when she's here — it's not that. But you're young. Have you ever been with a woman? I'm sorry. I shouldn't ask. But you probably don't know the degree to which women can feel threatened, and for absolutely no reason whatsoever! It's almost as if it doesn't matter whether the threat is real or not, it's the *perception* of a threat that moves them the most. I think women are more interested in having control of a man's mind; men like to control a woman's body. That's why it's always wise, when she asks you what you're thinking about, to say, "Oh, nothing." Or, "You, dear. I was thinking about you." Don't even get started. Word to the wise. Because once she gets a foot in the door of your mind, it's all over.

Thinking back to what happened, it's just — one ends up avoiding the painful moments, in memory. There's even a desire to change the way it *really* was, in our minds, to make it easier, less painful to remember. One wants to think back on that year as if the Watermelon Festival happened as it always had. I even want to see your mother there, watching from the sidewalk, or perhaps taking part in some small way.

Perhaps if the choice of king had been different. I was among those — the elders — who would choose the man that year. Me — an elder. Hard to believe. We had yet to choose when she came, but I think we all knew whom it would be. We had to cart out the swamp woman, of course, but we all knew. We were running out of options. No one is a virgin anymore, Mr. Rider, and this had become our biggest problem.

Anna Watkins, Former Waitress

Anna Watkins had long brown hair, which she braided like bread and let hang down her back. A tall, thin woman almost never without a smile, she had, still, the dark happiness of a survivor. She no longer lived in Ashland when my talks with her took place, but she remembered her time there clearly and seemed eager to share her story with me. Sometimes she would reach out and grab my hand, as though, as she wandered back in time, she felt as though she were falling backwards herself. And when it became too hard and she closed her eyes to cry, I would say, "I'm just doing my job," and she smiled and said, "Good detective." She was one of those people, to me, that we haven't made a word for yet. Not mother, not sister, not friend: she was a little a bit of each of those put together. I'm still trying to figure it out. Detective, I think, is just another word for storyteller: it's a way of making sense of things after the story that you're telling has already taken place.

I met your mother when I was eighteen years old and working as a waitress at the Steak and Egg, every morning serving coffee to anybody who had fifty cents and a shirt and shoes on. Dark days, for me, before she came. I mean, there I was, a high school graduate, without much hope that things would ever change. I would always think about how many actual *cups of coffee* I'd poured, and I thought, *I can't count that high.* And if I could have and had actually arrived at the number, I thought I might have to kill myself. It would have been too depressing because it would have been the biggest number there was in my life up to then. I had probably served more cups of coffee than I had dollars in the bank. More cups of coffee than kisses from a man. More cups of coffee than times I had told my nephew to straighten up and fly right, or told Janet, my best friend from high school, to leave her own husband because he was just no good. I had served more coffee than mornings I'd slept late, than men I'd admired, than long walks on the beach and free gifts and tears shed and more times than I had thought about getting things over with altogether.

Actually, I'd only thought about that a time or two, not because I really wanted to — not anymore, certainly, and not for a long time, don't worry yourself about that — but because I wondered how I would do it if I *did* want to. And there didn't seem to be an easy way, really: hanging, shooting, cutting. They all seemed very difficult. Pills and liquor were the attractive alternative, but there was a high percentage of failure, I thought, with that method. This is why people who do kill themselves must be really serious about not wanting to live, to be willing to go through whatever, you know, the shooting or the cutting, to get *out* of this life. I had the need to escape. Thankfully, not from this life to the next, but from this life to another one. But for a while there it seemed like I had absolutely no reason to live.

Lucy Rider was a reason to live, or at least, you know, a reason not to kill yourself. Myself. Ourselves. I thought about it that way sometimes too: what would I be missing if I died? What? Sunshine and the smell of bread and — well — coffee? Sure. You could make a list. I did that, made a list of reasons to go on, of what was special. And Lucy Rider: she was on it. She would have been on a lot of lists in Ashland, years ago. I don't know that she'd make them now, but back then she would have been among the reasons to live for lots of people, because . . . oh, various things. Even her freckles. She had the best freckles. Sort of orange, sort of pink. I could go on about her freckles.

She was my friend, Thomas. Like a little sister. I know that over time you can make people bigger and better in your memory than they actually were. But in my mind now she is like the Statue of Liberty.

By this time she was settling into that shack we called the Hargraves place and was working on it. She'd gotten a handyman, Jonah Carpenter, to do the work. Jonah was an old, part-time drunk, but good with a hammer. She was paying him with sandwiches, but after a while he needed some money too. That's when I met her. She worked the morning shift with me at the Steak and Egg, until she started in with Iggy, anyway, and got the money jar. Good thing too about that money jar, because she wasn't the best waitress. She was lucky to get the coffee in the cup.

But anyway, that's how we met: me thinking about killing myself, and her trying to figure out a way to live. She was a good friend, Thomas. My best.

Iggy Winslow

I've had happy days, I guess. But the best, the number one? That would be when I came to understand your mama was starting to think of me when I wasn't around. I was proud. I knew that was happening because she came right out and said it. She said, "I've been thinking about you, Iggy."

"And I've been thinking about you too, Miss Rider," I said, but still, something told me that we hadn't been sharing the exact same thoughts about each other.

"You know what I've been thinking?"

I said, "No ma'am."

"I've been thinking about how nice it would be — how really nice — if I could teach you to read."

"Oh, is that right?" I said, and I took a backwards step or two, because in the nature of our thoughts about each other we couldn't have been much further apart. As she talked, things slowed down, and each word took its own sweet time in making its way into the world until that first part — *I've been thinking about how nice it would be* — set out there real nice and perfect because I'd been thinking about how nice it would be too. It was a cliffhanger, though, what was coming after, and when she said what she said — *if I could teach you to read* — well, I'd be lying if I said my heart didn't sink a little. My heart sank a little. Of course, my heart might have stopped if she'd said what I'd wanted her to. Sometimes the worst thing in the world is for a man to get what he wants — that's what my mother said, and I always thought she didn't know what she was talking about. 'Cause I would have been happy to die then, getting what I wanted, knowing Lucy Rider wanted me. It would have been a nice ending to a sorry life.

As it was, I lived, and right off started learning to read. She had discovered I couldn't by leaving me a note one day. I'd seen her at the Steak and Egg the day before, and told her how I was coming by the next to mow her lawn, and she wasn't there, but there was this note on the door with my name in big letters at the top, which I could make out. But the letters after that I had no idea, the sounds they made in their particular group. I stayed with that piece of paper a long time too, sitting on her porch, like a time was going to come and it was all going to make sense to me and I would look up at the little piece of paper and understand. But it never happened. So I had to think, *hard,* wondering what it is she would be writing me about, and I decided she had a few extra chores and whatnot written down here, something I could do if I finished real quick with the lawn, because it didn't need much mowing — it was looking pretty good with all the special attention I'd been giving it. I had to decide what chores she'd want done, and I looked at the house and thought, *Well, it wouldn't hurt to fix up the windows a little bit, rip some of those clinging vines off the screens, trim up the shrubs.* Shrubs have a way of getting ratty if you don't watch out. So I set to work, and by the time she got back I'd pretty much finished up. I was just sweeping some of the cuttings off her porch when she walked up kind of slow holding a grocery bag against her chest with the top of it, the part of the bag that cuts you sometimes, grazing her chin. "What happened to my shrubs?" she said. "And my lovely vines?" Almost crying and upset with me, both. I pulled the note out of my pocket, where I had put it for safekeeping, and I uncrumpled it and looked at it and said, "Well, maybe I missed what you were getting at here," and she said, "Iggy," the whole truth of the matter clear as sunshine to her. You could tell by the way she said my name, all soft and pitiful like I was a dog who'd gotten into the garbage again. "I was just asking you to stay for lunch." Which was kind of a good-news-bad-news thing, because after all that work I was mighty hungry.

So after lunch that very day she started teaching me to read. We worked on it almost every day after that. We worked on whole words and we worked on just plain sounds, so I could recognize them in any situation. She had easy-to-remember rules like, *When two vowels go walking, the first one does the talking.* Once-upon-a-time stories. Once upon a time this and that. She was a *good* teacher too. I started learning real quick. I shocked Anna Watkins good one day when I sat down in her section, opened the menu, and read off the lunch special, which is different every day and new to everybody, and she just about had a cow. I still remember what the special was. *Ground beef patty with carrots and rice.* They still have that sometimes, and when they do, every time I see it there on the menu, I think of Lucy, in addition to all the other times I already do, which makes it most of the time, I guess. I'm thinking about her most of the time, to this very day.

Anyway. When it got around, what she was doing to help me, the town set up another money jar at the Steak and Egg for her. People just dropped in money when they had it, like they did for me, because they figured it was a service she was doing the town, making it so I could read and maybe do other things besides mow lawns, and then maybe write and keep books and make a real business out of what I do, which is what I did. I got an office and everything in the minimall. IGGY'S. Painted on the glass door in white paint. HANDYMAN, written below it.

But I'm getting ahead of myself, aren't I? And this isn't what you want to hear about anyway. You want me to get to the good part, the heart of the matter. Just what happened with me and your mother.

I can see right through you.

Betty Harris, Widow

Betty Harris, sixty-three, flagged me down at the Steak and Egg be-
cause she heard I was talking to people and said she had a story. She
lived in the basement of her first cousin's house, a mile or so away from
the tracks. Since her husband died in a construction accident, she'd had to
rely on the kindness of relatives to maintain herself "in the style to
which I am accustomed," which, she said, "is like an animal, but with
indoor plumbing." Her little apartment was dark and unkempt, and the
ceiling seemed unnaturally low. She was dressed in a maroon pants suit,
and her short black hair was brushed back and steadied with an indus-
trial-strength gel. She had a small, sour face. She smoked incessantly,
and when her lips gripped the cigarette filter they pushed out and sur-
rounded it, engaged it with such strength and intensity that she appeared
to be sucking more than just smoke from it.

Pardon me getting right to the point, but your mama was a
Bitch. That's capital B, i, t, c, h, as I see you're taking notes.
Be sure to write down what a dump this is, okay? Millie thinks
she's doing me a favor, letting me live down here with a hot plate
and the minifridge. I feel so blessed, especially when it floods, as
it does every damn time it rains. And you have to like the crick-
ets. If you don't, it just turns you sad and bitter, and I refuse to
become that! I refuse to let the circumstances of my life, over
which I have had precious little control, turn me into the kind
of woman you see sometimes with the thin lips, pressed hard to-

gether, never smiling. I can smile. See? I just smiled. Let Millie think she's going to heaven because she gave me her basement. I'll see her in hell and I'll still be smiling.

Back to your mother, who, as I said, was a total bitch. She caused a lot of grief in this part of the woods, some the way it happens without thinking about it and the rest with the glee of a pyromaniac with a box of matches. My husband, the one who fell out of a second-story window a few years ago? He was a casualty of your mother. See, she was the kind of woman who got what she wanted by flashing a smile and a promise. She gave men hope. *Maybe if I just build her a deck on the back of her house, maybe while I'm out there she'll bring me a lunch* — she was *famous* for her lunches — *and we'll sit and talk and one thing will lead to another.* And maybe I'll find a lump of gold in the mashed potatoes. Maybe one thing would lead to another, and it did — I imagine on occasion it did. But there weren't enough hours in the day to cash in every rain check she gave out. Carl, bless his heart, was just a man. You couldn't blame him for failing me and himself the way he did. You could make him suffer — and I did — but you couldn't blame him. He was like a pitiful beat-up dog.

See, Carl didn't have any real talent to speak of. He couldn't build a deck. He didn't know anything about plumbing. He didn't even have both eyes — his left one was glass, because he got it poked out when he was a boy, falling on the top of a metal fence. He only did construction because he was strong enough to lift heavy objects. But there were all these men getting to hang around old Lucy because they could *do* something, help her out and all, and poor Carl catching a whiff of all that excitement and not being able to cash in — that hurt.

Then word got around that Lucy was teaching Iggy Winslow to read. That's when it all hit home for Carl. Never being much on reading, as I recall, he suddenly felt like he too needed to improve his skills. I said, "You read fine, Carl." And he said, "There are parts I just don't get. In the newspaper and stuff." And I said, "Well, maybe you should skip those parts." And he said, "That's what I do now and I don't want to. I want to get those parts." So he asked Lucy if she would help him learn to read better and she said she would be happy to, and they set up a time because Lucy had *all the time in the world,* not having to work a real job and getting all that money from the jar at the Steak and Egg. They set up a jar for me too after Carl died, but it dried up after a couple of months. Lucy kept that jar full nearly a year.

So Carl came back from his first reading lesson and I could tell he had fallen in love with your mama! He had the goo-goo eye and the red cheeks, and he looked away every time I mentioned her name, as if he had a big secret. A secret love. So I said, "Carl, how'd the lesson go?" And he said, "Fine. We worked on double vowels first thing." Then he recited this little poem. *When two vowels go walking, the first one does the talking.* "Makes it easy to remember," he told me, "about the vowels." And to poor Carl it was like a love poem. He recited it every day until his next lesson.

So it became a weekly thing, and every week Carl got deeper into the muck with her. Everything I said or did just became offensive to him. I could see him looking at me, comparing the way I was to the way Lucy Rider was, and it was not Lucy Rider who was coming up with the short end of the stick. She of the lips, she of the eyes, she of the hair. And it couldn't be helped, because he knew what he wanted, he knew what he wanted but could never have, and he didn't want what he had already, so it was a sad story from here on out for me and Carl, Mr. Rider. Very sad. Not that we were winning awards for happiness before, but the thing was, the problems we had? Money, drinking, temper problems? They were our own. We could handle those. But not our problems and Lucy Rider too.

Meanwhile, she starts to make this stink about the Watermelon Festival, about how it's stupid and old-fashioned and just not right, and how we should stop it or at least change it some — the oldest festival of its kind in the United States! — and make it more friendly to everybody. I had no idea what she meant. I was not alone, either. What did she have against watermelons? And who was this split tail coming to our town for a few months — out of nowhere, by the by? Where did she get off telling us how to live? Did you know she had a Negro come to her house one day, in broad daylight, and that the two of them had lunch on her front porch, laughing away like old friends for the world to see? People couldn't believe it. Half the town drove by just to see. And I don't have anything against Negroes or lunch or broad daylight either, so don't go writing something about how I'm an old such-and-such. It's just when you put them all together. That's where things begin to be a problem.

But Lucy had played things right smart. When she started going on about all this, the Watermelon Festival and the Negroes and whatnot, some people — read *men* — thought maybe she had a point. Maybe we shouldn't just dispense with her ideas out of hand, the men said. Think about it. At least, let's go on over to her house and talk about it late into the night and see what happens.

I'm not getting into all that happened with Iggy, because it brings me too much pain to think of what that did to Carl when he heard. Because, see: Carl was her student too. And yet she chose Iggy over him. Carl couldn't understand that. Carl being the big and handsome one, and Iggy being so small and retarded-looking. She could have taken out a gun and shot him through the mouth, and Carl would not have been more dead than he was after the Iggy thing. Of course, I knew what was happening, in Carl's mind and in his heart, and there was nothing I could do, because I was suffering too. It was her way of trying to wreck the festival — everybody knew that. But Carl only felt the heartbreak, and there was nothing to be said to him after that — except, you know, I did. I said things to him. I was his wife, I had the right. Not that it helped anything. When he fell out of that window seven years later or however long it was since your mother had come here and killed him, my first thought on hearing about it was to question why he had waited so long. He had given up the ghost so long before.

Vincent Newby, Negro

Though African Americans — or Negroes, as they were generally called in Ashland — made up almost one third of the town's minuscule population, they were rarely seen in the town proper, in the shops, among the white pedestrians, or at the Steak and Egg, drinking coffee before heading off to work. Vincent Newby told me that he was a retired truck driver, although the truck he drove, and still did drive, was no more than a flatbed Ford, older than I was, the engine of which cranked to life with great reluctance, much the way Mr. Newby got up out of a chair. He was close to seventy-five years old, a small man with hair that looked frosted on its ends. His face dropped in folded wrinkles, as though he were once a much bigger man, and I found out that in fact he was: he told me he had diabetes, and it's been eating away at him for years, whittling him down to his current size. His eyes were bright, though, and seemed kind, and he spoke very slowly, as though a thought arrived before every sentence, which he stopped to examine.

I had a *great* affection for Miss Lucy Rider.

She came up to me one day and asked for help growing her garden. Said she'd seen mine.

I grow everything in my garden. Flowers, vegetables — and watermelons, of course. I grow the biggest watermelons, with the most seeds of any in town every year — I *know* it — but I can't enter the contest because it's just not done. She'd seen mine, and wanted to know how I make it so beautiful and growing large, and when I tell her she can't believe it. I tell anybody who asks me, but no one ever asks until she comes here and asks me herself.

It's the animals, I tell her.

The dead ones. *Everybody* knew about this, because it's the way it used to be done by everybody, but there aren't that many people left who will talk about it. But I would.

You get your dead animals and you dig deep and plant them beneath whatever it is you want to grow, and whatever it is you want to grow gets twice as nice as it ever could. It's an old secret from way back. My family passed it down to me. We've been here since the beginning. It's how everybody used to do it when there were more dead things.

Seems like there used to be more dead things, doesn't it, long time ago?

Things live longer now.

Long time ago I'd be dead.

But back then they'd take every horse, every deer and cow they didn't eat, or what was left over from what they did, every cat and dog and whatnot, you name it, when it died they'd take it out into fields and plant it like a seed. And it *was* a seed. It *is* a seed. Not even death can stop life, if you know the secret.

They say even our ancestors, all of them, they were buried out in the fields too, and that's how come we got the watermelons we did back then, with the blood and the bones of our own people. Dead mules too.

And Miss Lucy Rider is looking at me with her pretty mouth hanging open [*laughs*]. But . . . she said, where do you *get* these animals, she asks me.

I tell her, Don't look at me!

I tell her, God does it.

I tell her, Sometimes your own little animal dies and sometimes you find them on the side of the road. That's where I find them lots of times. Raccoons and possums mostly, but dogs and cats too, wandering around too long. You get 'em and you bury 'em in your garden.

I had an old dog named Mike, and now he's growing the nicest yellow squash you ever seen.

Size of my foot.

She shakes her head, and I can tell what she's thinking, but she's just too much of a lady to ask. So I say it myself.

I'll bring you some if you want, I tell her. Not meaning the squash, of course. Meaning the animals.

Would you? she says.

I would.

That's how we got to be friends. I brought her the animals. I was lucky because this was spring and the little critters are trying to get from one side of the road to the other in spring. Seems like that's where love always is: on the other side of the road. So they're everywhere. I go out and shovel 'em into the back of my truck, keep a few for myself and take the rest up to her place, the Hargraves place, and plant 'em in the back where she's tilled the soil.

The last garden I ever figure to be in in this life is Hargraves's. His son killed my cousin years ago — did you know that? But there I am, in the backyard, planting a possum and a cat for a white woman.

You can't tell a story like this and have anybody believe it, but there it was.

I brought 'em around dusk. Sometimes she'd be teaching Iggy to read, and sometimes not. Sometimes she'd be all by herself and come out to the garden with a nice cool glass of lemonade and a plate of cheese and crackers, her big red hair pulled back in a barrette, and the matching freckles — I called her the Girl with the Matching Freckles — up and down her arm and on her cheeks. They made her look younger even than she was — fresher.

I liked those evenings. They were sweet, the two of us just sitting there, not talking, while I buried a possum or something. Once — more than once — her hands would start shaking, or she'd get real achy and tired.

I saw in her the same bad blood I had in me.

I've seen lots of things. Saw her reading with Iggy and that Carl. Through the window. I glanced in on occasion. Sometimes she'd be laughing with him. Then sometimes he'd be doing something to try and make her laugh but she'd be sitting there not laughing. I turned away and buried what I come to bury real quick, because I grew up hearing stories about black men killed for seeing a white woman like that, even just sitting with another man, not that Miss Lucy Rider would have me killed but that man, those men, I didn't know about them.

Well, spring turned to early summer and the roads were thinning out, and none of my animals were looking sick, and a couple of weeks pass with nothing dead at all, and I get all sad without knowing why.

Then I know it's because of her. I want to be near her. You know, just close, in her yard, talking or not talking, seeing her doing something through the window and drinking a cup of lemonade. It don't matter.

It got to be so bad I didn't wait for things to die. I went out, ready to kill.

If I see a possum on a side road living his life I'd pull off and rumble through the rocks and dust after it. Got some that way too.

Then I nearly killed myself once. Near about ran into a tree one night. Stopped just in time. Sat there in the car thinking about what happened. Figuring it out. I figured I was in too deep. Not in love. Not in love with your mother. But when I was

a boy there was a spot in a bamboo patch I went to sometimes, to sit and think. No one knew about it but me. It was like sitting in a secret room. Sun broke through in jaggedy patches. And it was always real cool, even on a hot day. A good feeling, just to be there.

That's how it was with your mother.

Old Man

This is the story of the Dead.

We took them out to the fields at night. Our mothers and our fathers, our babies, our brothers and sisters, and eventually, we knew, ourselves: once we succumbed to age, to disease, accident, or if we left this life by our own hand, we too would be wrapped in a burlap sheet and taken from our casket by the hands of the strongest men and buried deep within the fields around our town. It all started when the old burying grounds began to grow lush with all manner of things. Flowers, vegetables, herbs. Whatever seed happened to find its way to this soil prospered like nowhere else, and we looked around us at our barren fields that were supposed to support us with their bounty but didn't, and we had an idea. With the bodies we grew corn, and tobacco, and cotton, but most of all watermelon, the crop that fared the best. They say that's why watermelon meat turns red: it's colored by blood, which the fine and mossy tendrils wrapping around our bodies would suck out and bring to the surface. And so within each watermelon was a little bit of who we are, or were, and some said back then you could actually taste it, at the end of a long hot summer's day, slicing through the thick green crust and bringing a slice of it up to your parched mouth and eating, they said sometimes it might remind you of somebody you once knew, or loved, or lived with, even, and lost. "Daddy," you might say. Or, "Sweet Sally." Or, tears streaming down your face, tasting and remembering, "This is my baby, Lee."

As with many things in our town, what is known is often forgotten, or stored in the part of the brain that resists remembering. How else to explain our actions? Everybody knew we removed the bodies from their caskets, and that the box they buried on the morrow was empty.

We still prayed and cried over the nothing inside.

Iggy

I sat right at her kitchen table, elbow to elbow there, about as close as you can be to another person without sitting on her lap. It was slow going there for a while. I was supposed to be looking at her finger moving along the letters of a word on the page, and instead I'd be looking at her neck, and her hair, and not listening so much to what she was saying as the sound she made when she said it, how pretty everything was when it came from her mouth. It was getting to be real hot by then — it gets hot coming on April around here — and she wore the dresses where her shoulders and her arms were all, you know, *open to the air,* and so I had a whole lot more of her not to notice if I was going to learn to read. And *smelling* her. It was hard to concentrate, is what I'm saying, so I was not your best student, and it was slow going there for a while. That's all I'm saying.

But we kept at it. First I was coming every other day. Then it was every day. She wore my brain out. Sometimes, after, I'd go home and fall asleep on my couch, the fan blowing on me directly, and wake up not knowing what time it was and not remembering what it was we'd even studied. We were into it for several weeks before it started getting to me that I was not learning to read at all, and there were days you could tell she was losing her patience, and that if I didn't learn she'd probably give up on me, and then I'd be back to just mowing her lawn. A whole part of my life would be over. I went out with my mower one day, pushing it down Main and then up Fourth looking for a lawn, trying to keep busy and not think so much, and I came to the red and white sign at the cross street, and I looked at it. I said, "Stop." I *read,* "Stop." I put all the sounds together and made the word and knew I was right because it was a stop sign. I knew that much, of course. But I'd never made the sounds the word was on the sign. *Stop.* S-T-O-P.

Words start jumping out at me after that. *Eat. Gas. News.* Let's see. *Fresh. Food. Look. New and Improved.* Whatnot. Just all kinds of words. It was like never noticing trees before, and then all of a sudden seeing them everywhere. All along I thought it was just her I was with, waiting for that moment when our elbows would touch. But it was more. I was *learning.* I began telling everybody I was learning to read, and I bet she did too.

Then came that night of my life that so far has yet to meet its equal, inasmuch as it was the worst ever, and if there is a worse night ahead I almost hope I don't live so long as to see it. It was the night I found out that the Watermelon King that year was going to be me.

It was like a nightmare — but I couldn't wake up.

I'd heard how it happened. It was always at night. You could be walking home, thinking about a movie you wanted to see or a candy bar and all of a sudden the men would appear, and over their faces they'd be wearing black hoods with little holes cut out for their eyes. This was so you wouldn't know who they were, but when they came up to me that night I knew who they were right off. At the time I had come across a book of matches, and I was standing on a corner, lighting them one by one. It's pretty, the fire in the night. I flashed my last match and looked up and saw Al Speegle, the pharmacist, Carlton Snipes, who was the high school principal then, and Sugar. The one in the middle, Sugar, was holding a kerosene lamp, shining a yellow light about us, and the other two were holding the swamp woman, who is the worst-looking thing you've ever set eyes on in your life. What was left of her. She was hardly even a whole person. I don't even want to talk about it. It's too awful. Her face and her eyes. The men were just standing there in their regular clothes — that's what gave them away — with the black hoods on their heads, holding that tiny old woman, so old she couldn't walk, and so small she was like a little doll in their arms, and for a second I thought maybe they were on their way somewhere, to get the next Watermelon King, and so as soon as I got my voice back I said, "Hey fellas. How goes it?" All upbeat.

But they were in no mood for conversation.

"Iggy Winslow," Sugar said. "Are you nineteen years, three months, and four days of age?"

I said, "I have no idea."

"We say that you are," Carlton Snipes said, and Al Speegle said, "So it is written." Which only means they been looking at your birth certificate or your family Bible, or maybe they just asked somebody like your mother. But by then my mother and daddy both were long dead. So long that I was beginning to forget their faces.

"Okay," I said. "I'm nineteen and something. Why do you care?"

"And it is also known that you have yet to be with a woman, to sow your seed in the furrow of her fields" — I could tell this was stuff they memorized for the occasion, because they weren't talking with their natural voices — "yet to open the box where the seed is stored, that which is the beginning of us all, forever and forever. Is this true?"

"I've never done it," I said, kind of embarrassed, "if that's what you mean. You know that, Sugar," because Sugar and me talked about it sometimes, and he'd tell me when he did it, and what it was like and all. He was my friend.

And then the way these things happen, I knew for a fact what was happening to me, what they were doing, and how this was all going to go. And I looked from one hood to the other, hoping that something might happen to make it *not* so, like Sugar might say, "We're just practicing, Iggy," or something, but I knew that was just a wish without wings, that's what my momma called it, a wish without wings. I know it was me who was going to be king this year.

But then I remembered the loophole! And I got all excited. "Hold on," I said. "Just hold on. I was the oldest last year, too, and everybody got together and decided how it wasn't right to have somebody who was like, who was almost like, you know —"

"The town idiot," Sugar said.

"The town idiot," I said. "How it wasn't right because — what was it you said, Sugar?"

"Because you wasn't playing with a full deck," he said.

"Right," I said. "I'm not playing with a full deck."

"Because you can't even do the simplest things," Sugar said.

"That's right," I said.

"Like read," he said. "Because no one ever taught you."

"But I *can* read!" I said, not thinking now.

"Iggy Winslow," Carlton Snipes said, and Al Speegle handed me a little plastic bag with the hundred watermelon seeds in it. "You are the king," he said.

Then all of a sudden that old swamp lady started moving and I don't know where it came from, but all of a sudden she's got this watermelon in her skinny black arms, and she throws it at me like she's trying to kill me, and it crashed on the sidewalk and I was all covered in it.

And the four of them turned and walked away, taking the light with them, and I was left there in the darkness, holding the bag.

• • •

I'm not sure what happened in her life before your mama came here. But I know her heart was already full. I don't know what it was full of — love or loss — but it was crowded, and I got to say, she made room for me. There was a whole truckload of men in love with her, of course, most from afar, you know, looking but not touching, wishing without wings. There was some who touched too, more than a few, really, but they just touched the outside parts, her arms, grabbing her, *embracing* her — I seen it happen myself. I seen men coming by time and again. Like my daddy said, "The taste of the puddin's in the eating." They wanted a taste, a real good dollop, but I don't know as this ever happened. Not on my watch. But on the backs of some of the paper we used to write on, along the corners and the edges, she'd draw these little broken hearts, one after the other, and pictures of flowers growing, but instead of flowers at the end of the stalks there'd be cracked and broken hearts again, and hearts intertwined and the like. Sometimes she'd be drawing and not even hear me come in for our lesson, and look up all surprised and say *Iggy*. Like we hadn't been meeting at the same time, same place for months.

So I'd say she had her mind on other things. I did too, after the night I became the king. But she was better at setting her mind on the job before us than I was. I couldn't let go of what lay ahead for me, and that one reason — not the *main* reason, but one reason — it was happening was because of her and my learning to read. After that night it was like I tried to go back to where I was before we even started. All of a sudden I couldn't read the words I already knew I'd known. All the week before we'd been working on the *tr* sound — you know, like in *train* and *track* and *try* — and she'd even made me what she called her special treat, for doing a good job (it was a cheeseburger) — and then when it came time to read a word it was like I had never seen those letters before in my life. She said, "Try again," and I'd look and *try* again and nothing would happen. It was like she was asking me to pick up a car. My whole head felt tired from the strain, and she kept pushing me, and I kept not reading, and finally a little tear escaped from the corner of my eye and dropped onto the lines of the paper, right onto the letter *R*.

She said, "Iggy, is there something wrong?"

I couldn't hold back. I said, "Miss Lucy, I guess there is."

She didn't like that I called her Miss Lucy, but everybody said this is what I should call her, so I did.

"Do you want to talk about it?"

And I said, "I do."

She knew about the Watermelon Festival. I remember her getting all excited a while back about guessing the seeds in the Big Watermelon. She was like a little girl about it. And she had volunteered to help with the Daughters of the Confederate Dead float — she was a part of everything then, the whole life of the town. But she didn't know about the king — it was not something we just come out and tell anybody — so I started in to tell her. The whole story, everything, ending at what had happened the night before, what with the men on the street in their hoods telling me the news and the woman from the swamp throwing down the watermelon.

I reckon I'd never seen her get upset over anything. Not that I knew her all that good, really. Not that I'd seen her be all the things she was. But I remember that day so well. She was quiet listening to me talk, but it was like I was speaking another language and she was having trouble understanding, because she looked at me with her eyes all hard and concentrating, the way mine did when I read, and shook her head, unbelieving, and then when I finished she almost couldn't talk.

Finally she said, "I . . . I can't believe this. Literally, it's almost beyond my capacity for believing. But no one could make something like this up."

"No," I said. "It's true. Every word."

"But to take a young man," she said, "such as yourself. And parade him about. And then his first sexual encounter is out in a field with someone — it's . . . *barbaric*. It's like the vestiges of some primitive religion or — it's terrible. It's just terrible."

"I don't know about that," I said. Because I didn't. I didn't know what some of the words she was using meant. "Really. It's just what happens. Some people are one way or some people are another, and this is us. This is what we do."

"Did," she said.

And I said, "Do."

And she turned to look at me, the way she did when she had something really important to say, and she held my hands in her fingers and said, "Iggy, I promise you: you will *not* be the Watermelon King. Not this year, not any year."

"And you know what has to happen?" I said.

"I know," she said.

She knew.

Al Speegle

It's getting hot, isn't it? Very hot indeed. Every summer it gets this hot, and then hotter, and yet we carry on as though this were the first time. In America, in Western cultures in general, the weather is seen as something *apart* from us, but the Chinese always knew differently. Perhaps that's where the phrase *Somewhere, a monkey's laughing* came from; I don't know. There are monkeys in China. They knew the passage of the seasons and changes in the weather could have a huge influence on the human body, its health and temperament. Wind, cold, heat, moisture, dryness. These were all elements the Chinese pharmacist took into consideration when prescribing an herb, or the root of some . . . rare vegetable. Not in the West, however. Not in America. Not in *Alabama*. And certainly not in Ashland. When the summer comes, we rail against it, we complain, we wear our summer clothes. But we never *embrace* it. We refuse to *understand* it. Why did a town that once grew more watermelons than any other locality on the planet Earth suddenly, over a relatively short period of years, simply . . . and completely . . . dry up? And what compels a people, a coordinated citizenry of which I am a part, to maintain an almost ancient and pagan ceremony to "honor" a plant?

It's the heat, Mr. Rider. And, of course, the humidity.

In answer to your question, though, yes. As cochairman of the Watermelon Festival that year, Lucy came to me to discuss

Iggy's situation. She sat in the same chair you're sitting in now. She was quite indignant, I remember, clutching her purse in her lap the way I imagine she'd seen the older women do. My wife does it when she's angry. As though the purse were a talisman of some kind. And *very* serious, your mother — though difficult to take completely seriously. I only mean to say that she was an object of such beauty that it was difficult to truly believe *she had a mind*. Or a moral compass. Or anything else at all. How could she? Would God give one person all that? I think perhaps He did give Lucy Rider all that.

She came to her point directly. She made it clear that she found the entire proceeding surrounding the Watermelon King brutal and graceless. How could a young man be made to suffer, humiliated in front of the entire town, simply for maintaining his chastity, a choice that would be regarded elsewhere as a virtue, something to be celebrated? She felt that Iggy, in particular, would suffer irremediable harm from being subjected to such a proceeding, given his physical and mental disabilities, and the way he was regarded within the community. She said, and I believe I can quote her here, "This is adding insult to injury. It is like a nightmare from which he cannot wake."

I told her I couldn't agree more. Having lived here all my life (and, by implication, though I didn't say so, not a mere three months, as it was in her case), I told her how I'd seen some men completely defeated by riding in that float pulled by mules, the watermelon rind cut to fit like a snug little bowl around their head, waving to the crowd with one hand and holding in the other that limp, desiccated vine. Even though the episode lasts only a few minutes, the effect upon the individual in my experience is from that point forward they bear on their shoulders an immense boulder, on which these words have been torturously etched, announcing to all who meet him, now and forever: *I was once a king.* Since that time he may have become other things as well — a businessman, a husband, a father — but he's never truly able to escape the designation that defined him on that dark and disastrous day.

That being said, I told your mother, the Watermelon Festival is a time-honored event in our town. It's part of who we are as a people. Someone once said that if one does not learn from the past, one is condemned to repeat it. Well, in our case, this is not entirely true. In Ashland, all we *have* is the past, and thus we strive to repeat it every chance we get. In Rome, Italy, today, as we speak, the government is corrupt. The air is polluted. The water undrinkable. Venereal diseases are traded like cards. It's a rank and disgusting place, believe me, Thomas. And yet do you think a day goes by when its inhabitants are not suffused with pride, at least momentarily, knowing the stock from whence they came, and that their wretched, dying little city was once the greatest power in the known world?

For years, we were once the greatest power in the world, that is, the greatest *watermelon* power in the world. If you wanted watermelons, and lots of them, you came to us. Period. And yet I don't see that a town such as Ashland has much to look forward to in the New Economy, Mr. Rider. We will survive, of course, but who really cares? Once you've known glory, mere survival is an insult, a provocation. While progress beckons us toward eternal mediocrity, we choose to look back, to a time in the life of our town when we were special, when we were unique.

I can tell you don't understand: what, you wonder, could a town like Ashland possibly hope to offer? And the answer is nothing — to you. Nothing to an outsider. There were never any great statues or art, no museums or commemorative coins minted, no special scent in the air that might indicate by its sweetness that you had come to a special place. The glory was in the knowledge that we and we alone occupied an extraordinary and singular place in the world. History and tradition is culture. We had a culture, and now it's gone. Iggy, and others like him, I told her, are individuals who must sacrifice for the greater good.

To maintain the culture. To be part of a town that was better than our very selves.

Your mother didn't understand. She was just a child, really, a few years older than you are today, and sacrifice is not popular with the young. So she said something offensive, then she stormed off, slamming the front door behind her. I hate to paint her in a negative light for you. I know why you're here. Our parents are always seen to be holding the key to who we are, something they did or something they were, and we think that if we can just dig deep enough into their hearts there will be something inside, something very much like a clue, evidence, a telltale sign pointing to who we are and how we got that way. That's why you're here, isn't it? The mystery that you're after isn't so much what happened to your mother, but what happened to you: *you're* the mystery, Mr. Rider, the unknown. We know who we were, but you — you don't even know who you are. That must be terribly hard for you, and sad, and I wish I could help you. Does it help to know that she was at times a very difficult woman? Perhaps you can now see yourself as a difficult young man.

It was disappointing to me, though, the way she stormed off. I liked being with her, and I had so much more to say. For instance, did you know the first recorded harvesting of a watermelon was nearly five thousand years ago in Egypt? In Egypt, watermelons were grown not only for their flavor but for their beauty. Men traversing the desert didn't worry much about the water supply if they had a watermelon by their side. In fact, when the children of Israel wandered the desert after their flight from Egypt, it was the watermelon they left behind that they thought most wistfully about.

The history of the world is our history too. Perhaps in this light she would have better understood. But I never got a chance to tell her these things. For it was not long after our little meeting that things began to fall rapidly apart.

Sugar

Sugar was a big man, fat in a powerful way, who wore overalls and an old green baseball cap on his head. His chin was lined with stains from chewing tobacco, the juice from which he could spit amazing distances. He showed me how far one day, and I told him I thought that was pretty cool.

For his best friend, I don't reckon I've been that good to Iggy. When we were boys I used to beat him up on occasion, I really got on him, just because I could. I spread rumors about him, like he didn't know where a woman's love-box was and so forth, and then of course I ran over his dog. But that was an accident, and I apologized, and I think he's all right with it now.

But coming up to him in the night with the hood on and handing him the bag of seeds — that was the worst thing, by far. Here's a boy who lost both of his parents in a car accident when he was ten years old. They drove off a bridge and drowned in the Warrior River. He didn't have any brothers or sisters because his parents stopped having children after they saw what the first one looked like. They were not the brightest people themselves. And drunks, both of them. He was cursed inside and out, and the doctors said it had something to do with the amount of alcohol his parents consumed before, during, and after he was born. Most of us have a face we can show to the world that hides our insides, but with Iggy it was like his face and his body were the same, all of a piece, one terrible piece. They took him out of the oven too soon, is what he looks like, all of his features so small, some nearly not there at all. He doesn't even have his little toes, not on either foot. I don't know how many people know this besides me. Eight toes: that's all he's got.

So I didn't want to have to do what we did that night, but as far as we knew — and we knew pretty good; it's a small town, Mr. Rider: people just know — he was it. The virgin. Everybody behind him was just too young. You can't get a little boy to be the Watermelon King. A mother is not going to have her fifteen-year-old son on that cart. So the question is, when does a man become a man?

It's not always an age thing. A man is someone who carries himself through the world as if he were a part of it. He's responsible for himself and his actions. You might be sixteen when this happens, you might be older — or it might never happen. You might never be a man. That's what we thought the case was with Iggy. Because he just wasn't all there.

Then your mother came and took an interest and suddenly we began to see him in a different light. Part of it was the fact that he was doing things he'd never done before. Reading and writing. I found a note on my door one day that said, "Call me — Iggy." Written on the back of an old to-go menu from the Steak and Egg. I couldn't believe he had done this, written this little note. It was the sort of thing a man might do.

The other part, and maybe the bigger part, is that, of all the men in this town who wanted to be close to your mother, Iggy was the closest. She had chosen him above all the rest. Others had their chance — she gave everybody a chance, face time anyway — but Iggy was the one she came back to time and again, and so not only did this qualify him as a man, it also made the other men a little bit jealous, and hateful. That is, if he was going to be able to claim all the good parts of being a man — and being elbow to elbow with your mother was a good part, one of the best we could imagine — then he was going to have to shoulder the bad part too. It was pretty much decided, and there was nothing I could do about it.

Anyway, Iggy was our last and only choice, and when your mother did what she did . . . Well, to put it mildly, it wasn't just Iggy then. We were all fucked. Each and every one of us.

Vincent Newby

Word travels right quick in Ashland, and word got around *real* quick about how Iggy was going to be the king that year.

Folks knew it wasn't right. Folks knew.

You could just tell.

It didn't matter what we thought about it, though, because you just go along with it. I don't know another way to go, do you? But people talk with their eyes, and we all knew how it was.

We be laughing though too. We be *laughing* at the white folks. And that's the truth.

'Cause I could of named *three* of our own boys right perfect to be the king, just perfect. But it wasn't like we were asked or counted. Because it wasn't like we were really people.

We might be eating and drinking and living and dying no different from them, but the way it was, them doing it and us doing it the same, it was all like a coincidence.

So it was sad, but we be laughing. We be laughing sad.

Carlton Snipes

Allow me to paint a picture for you, Mr. Rider. The Water-melon Festival Committee — that is, Sugar, Mr. Speegle, and myself — met every Saturday at four in the afternoon in the weeks preceding the event. Every possible detail was discussed and examined at our meetings: how many floats, for example, and who will be on them; invoices, so forth and so on. At one such meeting there was a knock on the door. It was your mother. She wore one of those dresses she'd brought with her, nothing you can get around here, a crazy thing, too short, of course, and the design — I will never forget — based on Monopoly, the game. It was covered with pictures of Monopoly money, the cards — Get Out of Jail Free, et cetera. She didn't wait for an invitation but walked right in, her business face on tight, nodding to each of us.

I said, "How can we help you, Miss Rider?" Though she'd clearly interrupted our meeting and her presence was *entirely* inappropriate, I was raised to be polite to women, no matter who or what.

"Actually," she said, "it's how I can help you."

She smiled. Al, Sugar, and I looked at one another with big question marks on our faces.

"Please, sit down," I said.

"Thank you," she said. "I need to get off my feet. I'm not getting as much sleep as I should."

"I find," Al said, "that I can get by on five hours' sleep a night. It wasn't always so. When I was younger —"

"Al," I said. "Miss Rider seems to have something to tell us."

"Oh," he said. "I'm sorry. Please."

She took a deep breath and let it out.

"Well," she said. "I have some important information for the Watermelon Festival Committee."

I didn't appreciate her tone. The way she said that: she was making fun. Of us, of the festival — of everybody, as far as I was concerned. Our entire town.

Sugar nodded, as though he were an important part of the proceedings. He had a nice big truck: that was the main reason he was on the committee. He could haul things for us. Certainly, it was not for his intellectual contributions.

"It's about the Watermelon King," she said, and immediately upon hearing this all of us shook our head and sighed, our patience with her and her little pet issue completely exhausted.

"Miss Rider," I said. "We've been over this time and again. I can't see that engaging us in this topic further will serve to do anything but waste your time and ours. We have important work to do, so if that's all you've come here to discuss —"

"There's been a development," she said.

This got our attention, somehow; seeing this, she smiled.

"The festival is only a week away," Sugar said. He looked at me. "Do we have time for a . . . development?"

I gave him a sharp look. Miss Rider continued.

"I'd hoped to dissuade you from choosing Iggy as king by appealing to your sense of reason. I failed. The truth is, I had something to hide. But as time goes by it's going to become harder and harder to hide. So I felt I should tell you now."

She paused, as if we should know what she was referring to. We didn't.

"*Please*, Miss Rider," I said. "Get to your point. We're busy men."

"Iggy," she said, "is not a virgin."

This absurdity broke the tension in the room like a popped balloon, and we all had a good laugh, Sugar especially. He went on laughing for some time. I had to give him another sharp look just to shut him up.

"Very clever, Miss Rider," I said. "I imagine this is something he told you during one of his 'reading lessons'? Came up in conversation, did it?"

"The thing is, Lucy," Al said, "men say that sort of thing all the time. You know. *Men*. Especially those in his position. It's just talk."

"Yeah, he wishes," Sugar said.

"At any rate," I said, standing to put an end to this visit. "Thank you for sharing. Now —"

"It wasn't something he told me," she said in a soft voice. She had this way of not raising her voice at all that I found unnerving. She had remarkable composure for such a young lady.

"You just figured it out on your own, did you?" Sugar said.

"No. Actually, it was something we did. Iggy and I, we — I never imagined I would have to admit to something like this, in front of three men, *but* — Iggy and I had intercourse. He was there, I was there. It was some time ago, actually. Two or three months. I hadn't wanted to say it like this — who would? But things have gotten out of hand and I felt, well, in the end, you can't have a king who is not a virgin. It just wouldn't be right. So I wanted to let you know. Before it was too late."

"I don't believe you," I said. "Iggy told us himself that he had never —"

"I made him promise," she said. "It was a mistake on my part. I was . . . I have not been exactly chaste since coming here. Who knows how many others I've saved from the same fate. But I made them all promise. Not a word to anybody. And Iggy kept his promise."

"It was not us who chose him," Al said. "It was the swamp woman."

"Clearly, she made an error this time. I understand she's quite old."

"Impossible," Sugar said.

"This is the truth," she said.

"I *still* don't believe you," I said, standing above her, my face flushed with my temper.

"You don't have a choice," she said.

"But we *do*," I said. "Of course we do! You're hardly objective. Your position on this issue is well known. Clearly you'll say anything to get your way. With only your word to go on we'd be fools to withdraw Iggy as the Watermelon King. Especially now, at this late date. Al?"

"Yes," he said, as though waking from a slumber. "There's precedence in a case such as this, isn't there? Several years ago, remember?"

"Marty Atkin's first cousin came out and said the same damn thing." I was surprised Sugar remembered that far back; I was surprised he could remember what he'd had for breakfast that morning. "She was just trying to do what she could. But no one really believed her. Or Marty. I mean, come on. *Marty.*"

"This is different," your mother said then in her soft, even voice. "You see, I have proof."

"Pictures?" Sugar said and laughed. "Witnesses?"

"I'm pregnant," she said. "I'm carrying his child."

And she just sat there, smiling, her hands resting on her stomach, which was protruding, clearly, I could see that now, like a small mound.

I hated her so.

Anna

She was a crafty lady, your mother. She knew they wouldn't believe her unless she had proof, and she was carrying it. They still didn't really believe her, because in their minds — though they didn't know, really, because neither did I — it could be any one of a number of men. But the thing is, they couldn't know for sure until the baby was born. They'd have to wait until then and have a look at it. Looking would tell them whether it was true. Because if that baby was Iggy's it was going to *look* a certain way. So that's what they had to do. They had to wait. And so the waiting began.

Iggy

I reckon I knew I was going to get the shit beat out of me, and I reckon I knew that Sugar was going to be the man to do it. He'd been beating me down all my life; he knew how to go about it, so I figured he'd be over that afternoon and he was. He walked in my place and got right down to things.

"Hear you been doing more than mowing lawns," he said.

And I said, "I'm not sure exactly what you mean, Sugar." Him standing and me standing with him right in my face.

"That's what I thought," he said. "Lucy Rider said you fucked her, but we *both* know that didn't happen."

"Oh, *that,*" I said, and looked away, shaking. "I did, Sugar. Me and her, we sure did it."

He pushed me backwards. It wasn't a hard push but I am so small and he is so big it felt like one, and I fell against the wall and it felt like the whole room shook.

"I should have told you," I said. "I should have told you that night you and Al and Snipes nabbed me. But she made me promise. And I can't break a promise. You know that. It ain't in me."

He pushed me again about as hard as he did before, but as I was closer to the wall I hit it faster and this time it *really* hurt. The back of my head felt like it had been crushed. But it hadn't.

"You think anybody believes that?" he said. "Iggy? Do you really think that anybody believes you and Lucy Rider? It's not even funny. It's awful. It's awful to think of your ugly body touching hers. I can't even think about it for longer than a second. Tell me it didn't happen, Iggy, so I can get that picture out of my head."

"I can't tell you that, Sugar," I said, looking at him square now. "I know this puts you in a tough spot with getting a king this year, but I can't be king because I'm not a virgin, I can't be — you know how it goes. You need to find somebody else."

And that's when he started hitting me. I really wasn't surprised, but that didn't make it hurt any less. First he got me in the stomach, and when I bent over holding on to it he hit me in the face, and that knocked me out for a little while, because when next I opened my eyes I was lying on the floor looking up at him, and I could just tell he wasn't through with me yet.

"So tell me about it," he said.

"What?"

"You and Lucy," he said. "What was it like, Iggy?"

"Like it is," I said. "You know."

"I know I know," he said. "I know good and well what it's like. I've been like that with all kinds of women. Lost count by now. But it's over a dozen."

"I know you have, Sugar," I said, because he'd always like to point them out as they was walking down the street and tell me how he'd been with her and how good it was and all.

"So how'd it go? What did you do?"

"The normal thing," I said. "We just did it the normal way." And he kicked me.

"The way you do it," I said, tasting the blood in my mouth, a tooth I couldn't afford to lose coming loose. And he kicked me again. *"Stop kicking me, Sugar!"*

He stood above me, breathing hard, shaking his head.

"You think I like this?" he said. I thought he did. But he said, "I don't." Then he bent down so he was back in my face. I could feel his breath, hot against me. "I don't like this one little bit, Iggy. Snipes said I had to. Because there's a lot at stake here. You know that. The Watermelon King. It is a *great thing,* as hard as that might be for some people to appreciate or understand. And think about it: it's you. You'd be part of something bigger than all of us." Then he sort of whispered, looking at me like a friend. "If I hadn't been such a young, good-looking fool, I tell you what: I would have *liked* being the Watermelon King. It's an honor, is what it is. Think about it, Iggy. Think about yourself. You've got nothing. Nothing! People can't hardly stand to look at you, you've only got half a brain, and who knows what kind of condition the rest of you is in. You could be dead in a year and no one would really care. Sad as that is. Besides me, I mean. But what would you have to say for yourself? What are they going to write on your tombstone, I mean? *He could really mow a lawn.* Is that what you want? What about, *He was the King.* How's that sound? Better? So just tell me the truth, okay? And we'll keep it between you and me. You didn't really do her, did you, Iggy? She's saying that you did, but you didn't."

I couldn't breathe through my nose because the blood had stopped it all up. I opened my mouth and gasped. "I know what I want on my tombstone," I said, still lying there on the floor, feeling pretty dead already, or hoping for it, anyway.

Sugar nodded. "What is it you want it to say, Iggy?"

"A lot of stuff."

"Okay."

"It's going to have to be a *pretty big tombstone,*" I said.

"It will be," Sugar said. "The biggest, the best. What is it you want on there?"

"I want it to say, *Here lies Iggy Winslow. He wasn't much to look at, but he learned to read and to write and on one day of his life he was a king. It was the day he loved Lucy Rider, and she loved him back.*"

Well. He worked me over good after that. Not for Snipes, either. It was all for him.

Al Speegle

As a pharmacist, I was perhaps not *completely* surprised that the others looked to me for a solution to what appeared to be an insurmountable problem: with the festival now less than a week away, we had no king. Sugar was unable to be of much help; his talk with Iggy proved fruitless. And Carlton had snapped. First merely agitated, he quickly became *despondent,* as he realized that he had been beaten by your mother in the only way she could have beaten him. So it fell to me to deliver us, and frankly, I felt up to the task. I knew things. I saw the boys who slinked around the condom display; I saw the boys who didn't. I had a Rolodex. I had the trust of many mothers, who looked to me for advice, both medical and personal. I began to inquire gently. I had leads, but unfortunately nothing came of them. There were simply no virgins to be had, not this year. We had pinned all our hope on Iggy. I tried to make the argument that this was in fact a *positive development,* inasmuch as the lack of a virgin might be seen as the ultimate fulfillment of the original aim. But no. The Watermelon King was a tradition. We had always had a Watermelon King, and to pretend that we could even have a festival without one was preposterous.

"It's over," Carlton said, head buried in his hands. "All of it, over."

Honestly, I thought he was overreacting.

"What do you mean," I asked him, "'all of it'?"

But he just looked at me, as if he knew something I didn't. And perhaps he did.

For as my search for another virgin faltered, and as the news of my failure began to filter through town, it was as if a great black cloud descended on all of us, from both within and without. It was eerie, in fact. Suddenly, it was as if everyone *knew* there was no king, and, knowing this, felt the loss more deeply than any one of us could ever have imagined. We had been robbed of our Great Distinction. No matter that if it didn't happen this year it would have happened the next, or the next after that — who really knew? The point is that it *happened,* was happening, and we suddenly realized what it had meant to us, how important it had been for so long, this ancient tradition, its meaning derived not from the present moment but from the presence of the past in the moment itself. The Watermelon King was a symbol of everything we had always been, and without him, it seemed, we were nothing.

Then it rained. It rained as it never had. The fields flooded, of course, and so did many of our homes. Perhaps this was the beginning of the disease that killed our crops. The downy mildew spread like a curse. One morning the watermelons seemed fine, and the next the leaves turned purple, then brown. Thousands of watermelons died, and those that didn't had a weird sulfuric taste, as if they'd been poisoned.

This is how it happened. The festival was canceled. Main Street looked like a dark alley in what should have been our finest hour. And there was not even talk of resuming the festival the following year, for there was still no virgin, and even if there had been, we knew it was too late, there was no going back. The heart of it had been ripped out. Had we decided to go ahead with it, without the virgin, without the watermelons, we would have turned it into something of a *historical reenactment,* the way men dress in gray and visit sites from the war, and fight the battles again that were fought there over a hundred years ago. This is what it would have become. But this is not what we wanted. We wanted it to be real.

As you can imagine, in our situation, we looked for someone to blame. Emotions ran high. There were no more virgins. But we were still hungry, I think, to sacrifice something.

Anna

When she told me what she planned to do I told her *Lucy, I said, you're opening a big box of things and you don't know what's in it.* She said she knew there was going to be fallout. She said, *I'm going to make myself scarce for a few weeks,* which was hard for her because she was such a social person, you know, always walking around town talking to people, helping them out if she could (and them helping her out in return). *I'll disappear for a few weeks,* she said. And I thought maybe that was optimistic. *People don't forget that easily,* I said. I said, *We're still fighting for something around here that started over a hundred and something years ago.*

Not forget *then,* she said. *But* forgive, *understand.*

That's when I realized why I had been so sad for so long. It wasn't that I was lonely, though I was. It wasn't that I wanted a better job, which I did. It was because of the South. I hate the South. I still hate it. I hate the long hot summers, and the pine trees, and the places where the pine trees used to be: the ugly strip malls and the 7-Elevens and the fast-food joints. I hate the little towns where nothing's happened in a hundred years, towns like Ashland, and I hate the crazy people who live there. Don't talk to me about that Southern Charm or hospitality: I hate it, because it masks contempt. I hate the stories we tell each other about *how things used to be,* about Me-Maw and Pe-Paw, and the farm and the flag and the war, and *Christ* — I guess I hate him too. Don't get me started. It's like living in a nice house that happens to have a corpse in the basement. You know what I mean? Once you get used to the smell and the flies, I guess it's okay. What was happening to Lucy couldn't have happened anywhere else. I know that in my heart.

But she didn't. She didn't know what she had gotten into. You can't single-handedly destroy something as big as the festival and expect forgiveness. The strange thing was, even though I was her friend and she was mine, there was a small part of me that felt she had gone too far. The festival had been there my whole life, and as much as I hated this town I would miss it. I would miss it because it was what I knew. I understood why she had done what she had done, but still. It was hard, even for me.

Anyway, the plan was for her to hole up in her house until we felt she could come back out and resume her life. But that time didn't come. I'd pour coffee at the Steak and Egg and listen to the people going on and on about how change was coming, and how bad change was, and go back to her that night with some food and tell her *not yet, Lucy, not yet.* This hurt her. It just robbed her of her spirit. Her face turned pale, her eyes dark. She wanted so to get out, to see the people who she thought had become her friends. But people were saying the most awful things — I couldn't even repeat them to her, they were so awful. And the men, young and old, they were the worst. What with their smirking and saying how Iggy had gotten them off the hook. They were the only ones who wanted to believe Iggy had actually done it. I asked her once — one time. *Who was it, really? You can tell me.* But she just shook her head and smiled. The truth was not leaving those lips.

So time passed and nothing really changed except Lucy: she was getting bigger by the day. She had to have been at least six months gone by then. One night she got so sick, I worried something was wrong and so did she, and she said she wanted to go to the hospital, up at Kingston, and so I picked up the phone to call. But the line was dead. None of the phones in her house was working at all. She and I just looked at each other and she knew what was happening, and I knew too, and I said *Lucy* and she said *Forget it. It's fine,* she said, *I'm fine. We can do this ourselves. I know we can. I don't need a doctor. I don't want one. I'm fine.* She just switched over. It didn't take her half a second. When one road was closed she went down another, that was your mother. She said she'd been reading all about babies and how it worked and that getting sick was part of it. Books were stacked on her bedside table, and I looked at a couple myself. Good thing, too. She said she'd go to a doctor if there was a problem, but women had been having babies without doctors for thousands of years. Most times they just come sliding out. She called me her midwife. She was full of hope, that girl, and I told her so, and she said *Hope. Well, that was in the box too.*

Still, I felt like I had to ask somebody for help. So I went to Al.

Terry Smith

I felt for her. I really did. You know, I think I saw myself in her, in what she was going through. I had been there and back! *You're not so high and mighty now!* More than a few people said such things. Locked up in that house like a prisoner. It was a tragedy — really, it was a kind of tragic fall. A tragic fall from grace, a graceless, tragic fall. I mean, please, Iggy Winslow? The idea makes my skin crawl.

As a realtor, though, I'll be honest, I mostly had my eye on that house. She and Mr. Carpenter had pretty much restored it to its former beauty. White paint, black shutters, and (her addition) flowers in the yard. Her daddy would have been proud, I bet. It was very nice. I drove past it on occasion and admired it, especially after everything happened, and began to notice the strangest thing. You know that Hargraves story, about seeing his face at the window? I had seen that face myself. But now it was her. I swear to God. *Lucille* was at the window now, staring out. Every single time I drove by, her face was there, in the very same window Mr. Hargraves's face used to be, waiting for his boy to return.

It unsettled me, Mr. Rider. It gave me the scariest nightmares. It was like a vision of things to come.

Mrs. Parsons

People disappear from your life piece by piece. Even after they go they're still there, in memory, and then pieces of them go, one by one. I still remember pieces of your mother. I remember her hair.

I missed seeing her hair after she disappeared, missed it more than I ever could have imagined. It was nothing I could say out loud, though, because Tom — my husband — and the whole town, everybody was so dead set against her then. But I actually admired her. I admired her for what she had done. She was like me, she was like the me I wished I had been, feeling not her own pain, able to reach out to those who needed her. And Iggy needed her. What she did for him — whether what she said actually happened or not — it was a good thing.

I just wish I'd done more. Once, I took her a casserole. I left it on her back porch. I didn't feel I should risk actually talking to her. Someone might have seen me, and then it would have gotten back to Tom and things would have become unpleasant. It reminded me of how it was before, when blacks weren't allowed to eat at the Steak and Egg. Sometimes, the owners set out leftovers in the alley out back. There was a quiet, dark kindness in some places. This is what it had come to. Lucy was no longer a part of this town. She had become our nigger.

Carlton Snipes

No, I don't suppose there is much to say in regard to the next four or five months, however long it was, while we waited for you to be born. In a way we were all like children, eager for Christmas — which it turned out to be, of course, just about. The Watermelon Festival Committee members, along with a few others, met on a bimonthly basis to discuss the situation. The pregnancy seemed to be coming along nicely. Anna was a great help in ascertaining information; no one else had the access she did. She wasn't exactly a spy — I wouldn't go that far. But she answered whatever questions were put to her. It was through Anna, for instance, that we came to believe your mother would never leave Ashland, even in her condition, to return home or, perhaps, move on to some other small town she cared to destroy. Because Anna assured us that it was your mother's hope and expectation that she would one day be forgiven and welcomed back into the arms of the town, like the prodigal daughter. She loved us. This is why she stayed. It *was* touching, really.

But in the end that child — you — was not truly hers. It was ours. This was our feeling then.

It still is today.

Iggy

I don't know what to say about the rest. Me and Lucy kept up with our reading, and even more than we did before, because it wasn't like there was a whole lot else for her to do. She was all shut up in her house because nobody wanted to see her, that's what she said, and I couldn't say as how that wasn't true.

I never said to her what it was like for me. Various people took it upon themselves to beat the crap out of me, and those that didn't threw things and whatnot, and even the children took to yelling things at me when I was mowing their lawns. Some men, them that gave Lucy a try, or who said they did, they came up and winked at me and in a deep whisper thanked me for helping them out, because each and every one of them was sure that kid was his and never really believed I had anything to do with it at all. They said as much. But I laughed at them and told them that I did and how good it was and how she said I was the best she'd ever had, and they took it upon themselves to beat the crap out of me too.

She stopped asking about the cuts and bruises after a while, because it became an old story. One day someone got me with a bottle on my way to her house, though, and I was trying to cover it up but my arm was bleeding. She got some gauze and cleaned me up.

She was sitting there, her face close to mine, fixing me up. I couldn't keep the words down and out they came.

"Why'd you do it, Lucy?" I asked her. By then things had come down to a place so dark and awful I couldn't remember what the original idea had even been. She looked so tired and sick, and I didn't look the best I'd been either. It seemed like I had to ask. She took a while to answer.

"Because it was the right thing to do," she said.

I let this sink in. "The right thing," I said.

And she said, "Yes."

"Still," I said, "I don't feel good. Some of the time I do, but most of the time I just don't."

She smiled and placed the cool part of her hand against my cheek.

"You know, just because it's right doesn't mean it's going to feel good," she said. "Not at first. But later, when you look back, a person comes to see that they made the right choice at the right time and everyone is better for it."

"When is that?" I asked her.

"When is what?"

"The time for looking back."

"Ahead of us," she said. "That time is ahead."

But I don't see as how that time ever came.

Al Speegle

Anna came to me and expressed her concern regarding your mother and the child, but I couldn't say I had any experience giving birth to another human being. As a pharmacist, there are, *obviously,* a number of subjects on which I could match wits with any doctor, but actually assisting in the birth of a baby is not one of them. And yet I felt this is what was being asked of me. I had access to certain texts, and I spent some time looking them over. I learned, well, almost nothing, nothing that could be of any real help in the case of a serious complication. But it was comforting to read about those days before doctors and hospitals had become a fact of our daily lives, and to learn how, if the woman was healthy and the environment a clean one, a baby could be born and how both of them, mother and child, could in fact live through it. A baby, I learned, did not even have to be fed for days after it was born; as long as it was kept warm, and it was healthy, it would be fine. And I thought, of course! How were our ancestors born, after all? Seventy-five, a hundred, two hundred years ago. Where were the fancy doctors then? So I felt confident that I could be of some help. Unduly so.

I was called to the house and it was good to see your mother again. She was kind, as always, though by this time she had lost that . . . *spark,* you know. Her face was so pale, deathly pale, and her eyes were flat, like slate — they were almost gray. All her former radiance was gone. Perhaps it was all being directed inward now, to you. I don't know. But I brought out my stethoscope and listened, and I heard your little heartbeat. It was something. I told her it sounded fine, because it did. There was nothing to worry about, I told her. I visited her three times a week until the day you were born, and each time I told her the same thing. Everything was fine, I said. There was nothing to worry about. And as it turned out, I was half right, and I suppose I should give myself credit for that. But I can't. I just can't.

As it turned out, we should have called a real doctor. But things happened so fast. I'm just a pharmacist, after all. And as I said, I never even wanted to be *that*. I wanted to be a pilot, Mr. Rider. I wanted to fly.

Anna

Y ou were born right about noon, Thomas, the day before Christmas. A beautiful day. Sun shining down and warm for December. Her water broke about three that morning, and I called Al and he came over with his little bag of things and we stayed with her. It was a long, hard time. But your mother, she had a plan. All everybody had to do was live through that night and the next day, and I thought we could do that.

Of course, Al had to tell everybody that tonight was the night. He had to make his phone calls and we expected as much. Every few minutes a car circled the block, and lots of people — word travels fast — were taking early-morning walks past her place. Finally they gave up pretending and around ten that morning a dozen people stood in her front yard, just watching the house, like ghouls. It was like they were waiting for Elvis or something. It was awful seeing them outside watching. You knew what they were waiting on.

Al and me, we walked your mother 'round the house and up and down the stairs, because Al had read how this was supposed to make things happen a little quicker, and maybe it did. By ten that morning she was on her back in bed, and Al and me were beside her, keeping her face mopped with a dishrag and saying bright things.

That's when the bleeding started. Like a dam had broke. You've never seen so much blood. And Al's face: my God, he looked dead himself. But he got it together enough to tell your mother that this was normal, nodding and smiling at her, a little bleeding was a totally normal occurrence. This was not a little, though.

Al got out his stethoscope and listened, and played with a couple of the other medical instruments he brought. I don't know if he even knew what they did. But he sure acted like it, and Lucy looked like she believed in him. What I really think is this: she had given herself over to us. What was going to happen was going to happen. She wasn't going to fight it. All she could do was hope for the best. I mean, I was the one in charge of the scissors and the clamps for the cord. Me. So all she could do was hope.

But the blood kept coming, every time she pushed. It was like she was giving birth to blood and nothing else. I was down there at the bottom looking, wearing the plastic gloves Al brought me, and I saw it all.

Finally you started coming out. Using a flashlight I saw the top of your head. It was all wrinkled, the way the bottom of your foot looks when it's been in water for a long time. Lucy was screaming and Al by this time was completely useless, almost frozen in terror as you slowly came out. He held her hand, but it was more like she was holding his, getting him through this. And then when you came out, the cord was wrapped all around your neck, and your face was purple, and Al saw that and I think he thought you were dead. But I didn't. I read this chapter in one of Lucy's books. I got the cord off and clamped it, and then I cut it, following the diagram, and all at once, everybody started crying: me, you, her, Al. A quartet.

It was a mess. You were covered in blood and shit and I don't know what else, and I wiped you down a little but not much because Lucy wanted you in her arms, the little thing that you were, she naturally wanted to hold on to you first thing. So I gave you over, blood and all, the newest thing on the planet right then, and we all wailed together.

Seeing you here and looking at you now, it's unbelievable, isn't it? A man, from all that. It's like a magic trick. It almost made me believe in God, or some kind of Supreme Magician.

But not for long. Because the blood kept coming, and Al was already giving the baby the eye, nodding, saying, "There *is* a resemblance, somehow, don't you think, Anna? It looks a *bit* like the father, wouldn't you say?"

"That depends," I said. "Who would that be?"

And he nodded.

"He's a beautiful baby," I said. "That much is true."

And you were.

Carlton Snipes

I'm not sure how long we waited — an hour, maybe more. By this time word had gotten around and well over fifty people were waiting for the news, waiting for this birth and the reparation that was owed us. I don't actually know how many of them felt as I did. Some, as has been suggested, may have been there merely to wish your mother well. I find this hard to believe, after what she'd done to us, and those I spoke to seemed to share my feelings about it, at least peripherally. They wanted to see the child. They wanted to see the child and, having seen it, together, as a town, we could all agree who the father was, or, at the very least, who he wasn't. They suspected there was still one virgin among us.

But I had still other plans. In my capacity as chairman of the Watermelon Committee, I had come up with what I thought was a fair and equitable resolution to all our problems. Al Speegle was aware of it, as was Sugar. It was a radical plan, but I felt it was the only way to regain what we had lost.

It was actually quite simple. It depended on just one thing: whether you were a boy or a girl. If you were a girl, well, we were doomed, and we were meant to be doomed. But if you were a boy, we — the town of Ashland — would take you. You would become our king. Your mother could stay and help raise you, if she so chose, but in effect you would belong to us all, and *each year* you would reign as Watermelon King. This was my vision. Every year you would reign. *It could work.* I could see you, a little baby, and then as a boy, riding on that float in the parade, bigger each year, with the rind on your head and the vine in your hand, happy, waving to us all. There would be no "planting of the seed" for some time, of course, not until you became a man. But then, eighteen years later or so, you *would* plant your seed, and the child born of that union would take your place. And so on. We would have our king and our crops and all would be well. I realized that this was something of a perversion of the entire ritual. But times change, and we have to change with them. I saw this in my mind's eye. It could happen.

I must admit, I was feeling particularly good about it. Even giddy. Your mother thought she had won. She thought it was over, but it was just beginning. And so I waited there for the child. Al was going to bring it to me. He was going to swing open the front door to the Hargraves place with the baby in his hands, holding it above his head, and we would cheer, as we would see in this new life a new life of our own.

This isn't what happened.

He opened the door slightly and slipped through it, but he didn't have the child. People called out to him excitedly, asking him if the baby had been born, was it okay, a boy or a girl, and he waved at them, and held up a finger, asking for a moment, and he walked directly to me, where we stood apart from the crowd.

"It's a boy," he said, happily. "A healthy baby boy." His hands were shaking. His face was gray.

"And?"

"I was there," he said. "I . . . did it. I can't believe I did it, but I did. I was like a *real* doctor. Things didn't go perfectly, but I did it."

"That's not what I *meant*," I said. "You were supposed to bring the baby out with you. That was the plan. Where is the baby?"

"Oh," he said. "It's inside, with Lucy. We can still do the plan. But she wanted some time alone, with her boy. Some quiet time. I thought that would be appropriate. It is her child."

"Was," I said.

"Was," he said. "Was her child. Of course."

It was then I thought I heard a car engine, starting up somewhere behind the house. It could have been anybody's car, of course, but it concerned me.

"Is she alone?" I asked him.

"No. Anna is with her."

"You left her with Anna."

"Lucy," he said, whispering now, looking around to make sure no one was listening, "she isn't doing well. There was blood — lots of it. I'm not sure how much is acceptable under these circumstances. But she isn't —"

"The baby!" I said. "I don't *care* about Lucy. It's the *baby* we need, Al! Go get the child! If you don't, I will."

We turned toward the house, and he had taken only a step or two when the door opened. Your mother — it was your mother. Or what was left of her. Something had happened. It was too awful, seeing her that way. Even for me.

Iggy

I was hiding out there in the crowd when she came out, hoping nobody would see me. I had a sweatshirt hood up over the top of my head and I felt invisible and maybe I was, because nobody was paying me any mind at all, by which I mean there was no beating up on me and making fun. But I knew why that was. There was other things to see. Everybody had been waiting for this day, and it had come. I had too, I guess. I wanted to see Lucy's baby. I'd never seen one fresh. That I never got to see it is a regret, a sadness, and I wish she'd have let me in for a peek before the rest of what happened, but I kind of understand. It wouldn't have worked out that way.

So I was standing there with the rest of them, hidden away in the middle of the crowd when she come out on the porch. She looked awfully bad. Her shoulders all thin and weary, and her face — there was no life in it at all. Blood was all over the front of her nightgown. It was like she'd been soaking in it. It was redder than her hair. That's what I thought, looking at her. Blood redder than her hair.

Everybody got real quiet then, looking at her. Everybody, all the people in the town she'd come to be friends with, looking at her and thinking back — I know we all were — to those first days when she'd come, how it was all different then. And now looking at what it had all become. Because of me. I couldn't help but think it was all because of me.

Then she opened her mouth to talk. It was hard to believe she had the will for words at all. But she did.

"The baby," she said, "is dead."

And everybody sort of sucked in air real quick. I saw Al shaking his head, like he didn't believe it, and Snipes, his face dark and confused. But everybody else just in shock, seeing this ghostly woman on her porch saying those words.

"I want to *see* it," Snipes said then, his voice breaking into a place it shouldn't have: her quiet. "I'm sure I'm not alone, am I? No. No, Al here is with me. And the people of this town. All of us. We want to see the baby."

And she looked over at him all calm, and shook her head. He never scared her, not for a minute.

"Anna has the baby," she said, in a voice so soft it almost didn't carry. "She's taking him away. We'll bury him in my hometown. I didn't want him . . . here, away from me. Not in Ashland. Because I can't stay here anymore," she said, and smiled a little, a sad smile. "I want him with me, near me, at home. I'm going back too, when I feel a little better. But I think I have to feel a little better first," she said. "That's why I stayed behind. And to see you all once more." And she looked out at us all, her old friends who had quit her when she needed them the most. "To say goodbye."

Then she saw me. I don't know how, but she did. And I pulled my hood off so she could be sure. Her green eyes set on me and she smiled and raised her hand a little bit in the air, and I raised mine for her to see too. But I don't know as she saw it, because the effort of it all was too much for her, and that's when she fell. She just fell — not over, really, but kind of *into* herself, and down. It was like the strings holding her up had been cut. And that's what happened. She died, and the last thing she saw was me. That's the story of what happened to your mother.

Vincent Newby

I was out there watching with the rest of them toward the back and seen it happen, her coming out all bloody and saying what she said. People just frozen looking at her. Then, quick as all that, her falling down and the womenfolk screaming something awful, faces turned away like it was too much to take in.

Snipes got to her first. He held up a hand, keeping us back, because now everybody wanted to see. Mr. Speegle there with him, on his knees, touching parts of her, feeling for a sign. Still had the scope 'round his neck, and he used that too. People crying and not just the women either.

Someone ran inside for a sheet to cover her. Sugar. Then people started to clear out. Wandering away all quiet.

I stuck around.

Finally, it was just me and Snipes and Mr. Speegle. Mr. Speegle, I get my heart prescription from him. That's how we know each other. Snipes I know because he makes himself known.

I moved up close. I knew what had to happen. Everybody knew. No one said one way or the other — I just got a look. Snipes looked at me. Sometimes men are like women that way: all you need is a look and it's enough to understand, and that's the look I got.

I walked off and got my truck. Backed it up right to the steps. Everybody was gone by then. Everybody. They knew this was private work. I picked up Lucy Rider and she was so light she was almost not there at all, and I set her in the back beside the toolbox, still in the sheet. Then we drove off a little ways outside of town to the fields where the watermelons used to grow, and that's where I buried her. Don't worry: I made it all as proper as I could. I said some things. I made a little marker, but it's gone. I don't know where Lucy Rider is. All I remember now is how it was cold, and the ground was hard, and time I got home it was dark.

But that's it. That was a long time, the time between then and now. Since then, there's been a lot of death in my life. Birth too: my daughter had a daughter in that time. Big girl now, about your age. When they were looking for a name, I gave them one. Lucy.

Anna

It was a beautiful day. I drove south down Highway 31 with the sun flashing in the windows bright and winter-sharp. Behind me Ashland was swallowed up in the wooded foothills so suddenly it was almost as if it wasn't there at all, or so small not to matter, like a moment in time you pass through and forget, or like a dream you had that made sense while you were having it but in the light of day is impossible to make sense of, so you just put it out of your mind. I found that I could almost do this. Lucy was laughing when I left — crying too, of course, but the laughter: that was a good sign, I thought. I really thought she was going to pull through. No reason, I guess, no real proof. It was just hope. I had you up in the front seat by me and almost all the way there you slept. I watched you the whole way. Somehow I was able to do that and drive at the same time. You had started out kind of purple, but by the time we hit the highway you were pink, and I took this as a good sign. You were coming along, growing into the world before my very eyes. It was something.

Lucy had written the directions to her dad's house on a piece of blue-lined paper she tore from Iggy's workbook, but I didn't have to look. I had them memorized. The day before I'd gone out and bought a bunch of stuff for you: baby blankets, diapers, wipes, formula — and a little car seat, which swallowed you up. In case of emergency, there were also directions to Jefferson Memorial Hospital, which wasn't far away at all. I could have taken you straight there. But there wasn't an emergency — and thank you, to whoever's listening. We sailed along without a hitch, like this was the way it was meant to be.

I was not a big city girl, so you can imagine how coming into Birmingham and seeing all the buildings lurching up and into the sky made me feel a little dizzy! It's nothing to you I know, but it was like another world to me, even though I'd come down once before when I was twelve. Seeing something like that when you haven't seen it before makes you feel kind of distinguished, and I *felt* distinguished, and having you beside me made me so through and through. It was like a dream, driving through a dream, where there's nothing but you going through the world and the world is there for you to go through. I'm going on about it because there's not many moments in life that are like that, and they stick with you.

Anyway, after that there was a long stretch of country in the other direction. Then came the exit for Edgewood. It was a pretty neighborhood. The little houses, surrounded by big trees and green shrubs and all. Nice lawns. The house was just like she said, even though she hadn't seen it in a year, not since her mom died and all. It was on a little hill, and though the sun was going down it caught the last of its shining rays. I parked in front and looked at it, engine idling.

And this is where things got a little sticky. I was supposed to leave you right there on the porch. This is what Lucy wanted. Put him on the porch, knock on the door like I was the postman with a special delivery package, and then get out of there, because she didn't want him to know from anybody but her what had happened, what had been happening. She was right behind me, she said — it would just be a couple of days before she felt better and could come and he'd figure out what to do with you until then.

Besides, she said, *people leave babies on porches all the time.*

I said, *They* do?

In books, she said. *How many books have you read where someone opens the door and finds a little baby on the porch, all wrapped up and warm and wailing, with a note attached to the carrier?*

None, I said, *I've never read a book where that happens, but then I haven't read that many books.*

Well, it happens, she said. *Believe me.*

And I said I did. But I thought she'd lost her mind.

Still, it was what she wanted, and I was just the courier. I walked up to the porch and peeked into the living room window: I saw your grandfather in his big chair, reading a book, beside a pitiful little Christmas tree drowning in tinsel. He looked right ready to have his whole world change in the matter of a minute. So I set you and your things down on the porch and was about to knock and run. But then I thought: run to *what?* Back to Ashland? Back to the Steak and Egg and the coffee and the watermelons and not Lucy, because she was going to be gone soon, here or there, one way or the other? And when they found out I took you, what kind of reception was I likely to get? The choice had already been made for me, Thomas. Somehow, even before your grandfather came to the door, I had a feeling. And the feeling was *I'm not going anywhere.*

I knocked and waited. It seemed like I waited for a long time, but it was just that space, that kind of necessary pause, between the end of one life and the beginning of the next. I was waiting for him. He was a young man then, you know — quite a bit older than me, of course, but still, in the scheme of things, young. He opened the door and assessed the situation. Unknown woman with an unknown child. I didn't know what to say, and neither did he. We just looked at each other for a minute. And I could see where Lucy got her eyes. Then I moved aside so he could get a good look at you. And he smiled. I swear. Just looking at you made him smile.

"Your daughter," I said then — my first words to him ever. "This is her baby."

It's amazing how much a human being can take in. Here's a man who hasn't heard hide nor hair from his daughter in a year, and now there's this strange woman at the door with a baby she says is Lucy's, and how he can hear all this and see all this and not turn into a pile of ashes then and there is completely beyond me. But Edmund was special: I knew that from the get-go. He'd been through a lot already. There was me, there was you, and as it was starting to get fiercely cold out there, he brought us both inside and he made us some tea, and I told him the story, right there, every bit of it I knew. I told him about Lucy, and Ashland, and you. I told him how she would be coming along directly, in a day or so, as soon as she got her strength and saw a doctor, and he said, "No, I've got to go back for her myself. Now. I'll bring my daughter back with me tonight."

See? I liked the kind of man he was, the kind of man who would do that, on Christmas Eve. And he was almost out the door when I asked him, "Do you even know how to get to Ashland?" And he said he knew. And I said, "At least I can tell you where she's living," but he said he knew that too. It had been a long time, he said, but he knew.

Well, he came back that night alone. Lucy was dead and gone — literally gone — and no one could tell him who had taken her, or where. He tore the house up too, he said, looking for something, anything — a clue. But all he found was her charm bracelet on the bedside table. He brought that back, dropped it on the table in front of me. He had given her each and every charm on it — except for one. A little silver key with the words *To My Heart* written on the back. "Must have been from him," he said. And I knew who he meant.

Well, things happen, don't they? I don't remember if Edmund ever actually asked me to stay; I just did. He wasn't going to be able to take care of you by himself and go to work selling houses at the same time, was he? It just made sense that I set myself up in the guest room, with you sleeping beside me in the crib. Later on I graduated to the master bed. That made sense too. I believe it's true: you can make a family with whatever scraps you find lying around. And that's what we did. He wasn't my husband and I wasn't his wife, but it sure came to feel like that. And I wasn't your mother and he wasn't your father, but it sure came to feel like *that* too, didn't it, even though it was always just Edmund, Anna, and Thomas.

It was tough for us, though, especially for Edmund, having lost so much. If it hadn't been for you — laughing, crying, always needing something, food, drink, a diaper changed — I think he would have sunk into a place too deep to surface from. You were such a joy, but, at the same time, you were Lucy's baby, and she was dead, and to look at you was to think of her, especially in the beginning. And then later, after time made the grieving easier and Lucy became a little dimmer in our memories, I wondered what he was going to tell you — about you, about us. About her. It was something we talked about seemed like every few weeks. "I'll tell him," he said. And I said, "When?" "When he's older," he said.

Well, I guess you just never got old enough. But he wanted you to know the truth, as hard as that is to believe. Because I know I never knew a man less partial to the truth than Edmund. *Such* a storyteller! He always reminded me of some of the old country people I grew up with. That was part of his charm, of course. But it all comes from not being able to face the truth of his own life for all the pain the truth caused him. I'm a psychologist the way Al was a doctor, I guess. I do my best. And I guess I sound pretty smart. But it took me a while to get a handle on him. Years went by. Not that I ever *really* did. I mean, he'd be going on about Lucy running off with the circus, or lost swimming to Cuba, or whatever came into his head, *anything* — until, well, it was a Sunday afternoon. You know how sad a Sunday afternoon can be. We were lying on the couch, Edmund and me, plain exhausted. You were about seven. You'd been sick and he hadn't sold a house for a while, and outside it was raining. It was raining, but the sun was shining too, through a break in the clouds, and out of nowhere he said, "Somewhere, a monkey's laughing."

I said, "What did you say?"

And he said, "Somewhere, a monkey's laughing. It means —"

"I know what it means," I said. "It's what people say when it's raining and the sun is shining at the same time."

"That's right," he said.

"I just never heard anybody say that before," I said. "Except for people where I come from."

"Ashland," he said.

I nodded. He looked at me and I looked at him, the way people do at times like this. I'd grown my hair out, so it was long way past my shoulders, and he had lost most of his. He wore his Benjamin Franklin glasses, and that goatee — it made him look like a psychiatrist himself. But he was a realtor. The least likely looking realtor I'd ever seen, but a realtor.

He thought about this for a minute, then he said, "Certainly you're not the only people who say it, though."

"Oh. Certainly," I said. "You probably picked it up on an ocean liner, on a trip to Saudi Arabia or something."

"Or during the summer I spent working on that oyster farm," he said. "One of the other men might have been from Ashland as well."

"That was my second guess," I said. "But now that you bring it up — Ashland, I mean."

"You actually brought it up," he said.

"*Anyway,*" I said. "I've always wondered how you came to be the owner of the Hargraves place."

"I have several —"

111

"I know," I said. "You own property all over. But Ashland. Why Ashland? And that house, of all houses? It's always seemed so crazy to me. Like a real mystery. Why won't you tell me how you got it?"

"I thought I *had* told you," he said. He was one of those people able to look serious even when he wasn't. He had never told me and he knew it.

"No," I said. "Never."

"Well," he said, and lifted his head up a bit. "There a tale does lie. Believe it or not, I actually met the Hargraves boy."

"You didn't," I said.

"I did," he said. "After the *accident,* he left Ashland, of course, and, based on what he told me later, traveled a bit, working odd jobs here and there. Finally he came to Birmingham. This was years ago, before you were even born. I was working in a dry cleaners. He worked next door in a pencil factory."

"Pencil factory. I see. And what was his name?"

"That's the funny thing," he said. "He'd *changed* his name. To what I can't remember. But he had wanted so much to leave that whole world behind that he swore off everything from it, even his own name."

I nodded.

"And the house?" I said.

"I'm getting to that," he said. "At night some of the fellas, some of the fellas from the cleaners and the pencil factory, we'd all get together for a game of cards. Poker. *Serious* poker. The stakes got pretty high, for kids that had next to nothing anyway. I lost a car playing poker once. Another man lost his girl. Hargraves — or whatever he was calling himself in those days —"

"Because you can't remember," I said.

"Exactly. He had himself quite a hand, apparently. He was also a little drunk because he had just found out that his father had died. A lawyer had contacted him somehow. The thing is, you

112

couldn't tell if he was happy or sad about it. I don't know if there's a word to describe how he felt. Losing a father is hard, even when he was the kind of father Hargraves had. We'd all heard the stories.

"Well, I had a pretty good hand going myself. And the thing was, that day, I had just bought my first piece of property, a little stamp-sized parcel downtown. Not much, but it was mine. I had the deed and everything, and it got to the point where I had bet all my money, I had been seen and raised and raised again, until that was all I had left. It was between Hargraves and me by then. I threw the deed onto that pile and he threw his deed — to the house in Ashland — onto the pile next, and, sad but true — for him, at any rate — a straight flush beats four of a kind every day of the week. And that is how I came by the house in Ashland. In a poker game. And you know what? I imagine that's also where I could have picked up that little phrase. About the monkey."

"And you never saw the Hargraves boy again," I said.

"Never," he said. "But I would hear things now and again. He had a hard life."

"That's too bad," I said. "But lots of people do."

It kept raining outside; the sun kept shining. Somewhere, I guess, a monkey was laughing.

"The important thing is that things worked out in the end," he said, winking at me. "They worked out pretty well."

"I think so too," I said.

And I do.

TWO

"A long, long time ago, before the road came out this far, before man had planted his flag, by which I mean the 7-Eleven, up and down the highway, there was a swamp here, Thomas, and this is where you were born. You were born in the swamp, and accidentally abandoned there when the band of evil Romany wanderers who had kidnapped your mother packed up and left town. You had fallen into the roots of a giant oak, and the superstitious pagans thought you'd fallen through a hole to hell itself. But they took your mother with them, and later sent her to their ancient village in Aristea, far, far away, and where, through the power of her pure goodness, she became queen, changing the entire culture from the scourge of civilization to one of constant beneficent light — but that's another story, for another time. As for you, you lived for years on worms and the protein one finds growing on the back of water lilies, until I rescued you and gave you my name. Much time passed before you were able to speak the human language. You barked, mostly, but you could also understand the vernacular of the fishes, and you spent much of your time under water, which explains why you eventually became such a fine swimmer. Your grandmother would have been proud."

I grew up on a ten-acre patch of land quite a ways into the country. My grandfather called it a farm, but all we grew on it were pine trees. Blackberry bushes sprouted wild in the ditch on the side of the gravel road leading up to the house. We had three cows. There were no other kids living that far out, and my grandfather had to drive me two miles down the road so I could catch the bus to school. He would have driven me the whole way, but I liked the bus.

A woman named Mrs. Nevins was our only neighbor. She was older than anybody I had ever seen, hunched over, her skin papery and mottled, and every Christmas morning Anna, my grandfather, and I would go to her house to visit, and she would give me what she called a lucky dime. As far as I could tell there wasn't anything lucky about it, though; it was just a shiny new Roosevelt dime she'd gotten at the bank. So it was like a little tradition with us: every Christmas from the time I could remember we'd walk back from her house to the farm and all the way back I'd say, "I got my lucky dime! I'm lucky! I'm going to walk smack out into the middle of the road and not get run over because I have my lucky dime!"

Anna would laugh. But my grandfather would say, "Well, maybe that has more to do with you than it does with the dime."

"If she gave me ten lucky dimes," I'd say, "all I'd have is a dollar."

Edmund Rider — my mother's father, and, in many ways, my own — had a serious aversion to the truth, a predisposition to prevarication. I never believed a word he said. I was different from him. Even as a boy I saw the world in the simple ways it presented itself to me, simply as what it was. I was good at math. I liked the idea that there was one correct answer to a question, and that all the others were incorrect. But that kind of world was never good enough for him. That world merely provided the starting point from which he could weave his bogus tales of wonder. He used his power for good, though, mostly, and not for evil: he used it to sell houses. In this case, in the selling of houses, he never lied about the big things — things like plumbing or termites or whether the house was in a floodplain or not. What he lied about was the soul of the house itself: its past. Who had lived there before. What had happened there. Why had it even been built? These were the stories he made up and told, and they were so wonderful that you bought the house not because it was necessarily a wonderful house but because you wanted to be a part of the wonderful story he told about it.

He took me along sometimes, and I'd listen to him talk, as shocked as an eight-, nine-, or ten-year-old could possibly be, hearing these things.

This is him, selling one to a nice young couple:

"You may have heard about the great Tibetan monk migration some years back, when — No? Okay. Long story. Short version. 'Sixty-one, 'sixty-two? Sudden Chinese crackdown. Tanks, planes, bang bang, shoot 'em up. About a hundred Tibetan monks fled the country — that would be Tibet, of course. They didn't sneak. They were not sneakers. They were dressed — costumed, perhaps, is the better word — as an entire traveling circus. They were *flamboyant*. They pretended to be lion tamers, elephant riders, fire eaters, tightrope walkers. In their pockets, each of them carried a bag of Tibetan dirt. The homeland. The Chinese border guards — not as bright as you might think. They made it through without a hitch.

"And they settled right here in Birmingham, Alabama. How they got here, how they chose *this* city — that's a mystery. Except, perhaps, not completely. There are some interesting longitudinal similarities between Tibet and Birmingham. Some latitudinal as well. I'm not a scientist. Check it out, though. That's what brought them here at first. But then they were struck by the beauty, of course, the beauty of this town, here in the foothills of the Appalachians. And who wouldn't be struck? *I* am struck. Constantly. By the beauty of this city.

"Long story even shorter: this house, this street, this entire neighborhood, for a period of half a dozen years — completely

119

populated by Tibetan monks. Everywhere you looked: monk. Ellen, my wife — she passed away some time ago — ten years, hard to believe it's already been ten years — Ellen met them. She brought them cookies. That's the kind of woman she was, though. Gone now — Ellen, the monks — each and every one of them, but today people say this neighborhood, they say it's . . . blessed. And they must be right. *Because nothing bad happens here anymore.* No crime, no divorce, kids play in the street and nothing happens to them. Ever since the monks lived here and left. Eventually, they spread across the globe, those monks. Who knows where they are now. But in each yard? In each and every yard of every house in this neighborhood? A bag of Tibetan dirt. There is more of Tibet in this little Birmingham cul-de-sac than there is anywhere else in the entire world. Except of course Tibet. The light itself, as it flows through these windows, seems to have a glow all its own, doesn't it? Take a moment. Look. Really look. And the interest rates now, they couldn't be better."

He had a reputation. He was famous within certain circles, and not just in Birmingham. He made a speech at the Realtor's National Convention once. He wrote articles for the monthly newsletter. He said things like, "A realtor doesn't sell houses; he sells dreams." And, "Magic is your greatest asset." He never said, "Lie. Make things up. Whatever works." But that's what he was doing. Sometimes, when we were driving home together in the car, I would just stare at him, wondering where a man like that, a man who could say such things, had come from. And how I came from him.

The hallway closet housed his winnings, a collection of trophies and plaques. Realtor of the Year, Edmund Rider, 1977. And 1978, '79, '80. Other awards he kept at his office. One year he sold so many houses that he won the privilege of naming a street in a new subdivision. He could have named it anything he wanted to, but he named it after Ellen and Lucy. He called it Lucellen Lane. That street is still there.

People said he could sell you the shoes you were wearing, the shirt off your back, your own hairpiece if he wanted to. People said he'd sold Vulcan three times to some Japanese tourists. "That's true," he said, which meant, of course, that it wasn't. Vulcan, after all, was the largest iron statue in the world. It towered above our town, above everything except the clouds, on a sandstone perch atop Red Mountain. Vulcan was the Roman god of fire and forging; Birmingham used to be a big steel town, and Vulcan was built to celebrate that. Now there's no steel industry here, but there's still a Vulcan. It's like our Statue of Liberty, except Vulcan isn't a woman and he doesn't invite people to come live here. And I believe Edmund could have sold it. I myself would have bought anything from him, if I hadn't been who I already was.

"Okay. Seriously. Regarding the origin of you. Zeus came down to earth disguised as a cow. He just appeared one day out in the field. It happens more often than you'd like to think. Once, he came down to speak with your grandmother — needed her advice. On this occasion, your mother was there, helping out with the cows. And Zeus, well, you know how it happens. He seduced her behind the barn. The pregnancy was mystically accelerated, and you plopped out of her a few weeks later. In the old days that would have made you a demigod, but unfortunately all traces of any kind of supernatural power were eradicated in the public school system. Your mother was later taken to Mount Olympus as a kind of celebrity guest. She hit it off with Ares, and, well, she hasn't been back since."

He never answered my questions directly. He tried to be clever, and he often was, but the more he didn't tell me, the more I wanted to know. Who was she? Where did she go? What was she like? It felt like I was missing a piece of me. My life was like a book in which the first one hundred pages had been ripped out.

I needed a history, an idea of who I was. Everybody I knew had a mother, at school, on television. I wanted a story, a true story, so when someone said something about their mom, I could say something about mine. But he wouldn't give me even that.

Still, I loved him, and he loved me. For example: I was born with my right leg a little bit shorter than my left, so when I started walking, I limped. He developed a little limp of his own, just to make me feel better. So he had a good heart. His only weakness was lying. When he came home late for supper, it was never enough that he was stuck in a simple traffic jam. "A tractor-trailer loaded down with cypress logs jackknifed in the median," he would say. "The driver was fine, but his cargo wasn't. The cypress fell off the trailer and rolled toward the oncoming traffic, going thirty, forty miles an hour. Half a dozen cars were completely crushed, their drivers scurrying for their lives. It was a sight, let me tell you."

"*Cypress* logs?" I asked him.

"Cedar?" he said.

"Whatever."

A fact to him was like a rock in his shoe. He shook it out first chance he got.

"I sold a house today," he said, removing his tie, opening the refrigerator and getting a beer. *I sold a house:* he seemed to say this almost every day. He popped the top on the beer and ran it straight down his throat. You could tell it tasted good to him. I watched his every move as though I were from another planet, learning how to be human. I was twelve years old. "The little one I was telling you about?"

Anna, who had been listening to this conversation with her back to him — she was stirring something in a pot — turned around and looked at him.

"The one where the monarch butterflies rest for a night on their migration south?" she said. "Set the table, Thomas, please."

Anna wasn't my mother, and she never pretended to be one. But she wasn't like a stepmother either, because my grandfather and she had never married. He said he would never marry again, after Ellen. Anna was more like a much older sister, or an aunt, or some hybrid type of person they don't have a name for yet, and never will, because they only happen once. I set the table.

"So many they blot out the sun," he said. "Yep. That's the one. Sold it to a nice young couple. The woman had a little crush on me. You could tell."

"And don't you think they'll be kind of mad," I said, "when a year comes and goes and no monarch butterflies stop by?"

"They *could* stop by," he said. "It's possible."

"But they haven't, yet, ever, and you said they had."

"I did say that," he said, "didn't I?"

"You did."

"Because I could *see* it happening," he said, and he looked up at the ceiling as if he could see it happening now. "I could see them filling up the sky, blotting out the sun. They have come through here before, I think. Or nearby. Thousands, maybe millions of them. On their way to Florida. They'll just pick a place and settle for the night. On the trees, in the bushes, on the house itself. Ellen knew about butterflies. She loved them. She'd tell you it might happen. At night. After they've gone to bed. Leaving before morning. You never know."

"Still," I said, and he shrugged his shoulders. "I mean — come on, Granddaddy."

"I lied!" he said. "It happens. I come from a long line of really imaginative people."

"Liars," Anna said, looking from him to me, me to him. "You mean liars."

"What she said," he said, giving me a wink.

She didn't have to say it, though, because I knew all about that line. I believed in it as though, like green eyes and red hair, it ran in the family. And that made me think. Because if there was a line, wasn't I in it too? As his grandson, wasn't I at the back of the same long line of really imaginative people? The only thing separating us was his daughter, my mother, and I had never known her, and I didn't know anything about her, except that she had died the day I was born. Anna told me that when I was nine. I waited for more, but she said, "It's a long story, Thomas. But it's one I should let your grandfather tell. Ask him about it."

And I did, day after day. I had to.

I was a mystery to myself.

"People have been misled by that stork story for too long," he said. "I have no idea why. A stork is such an unlikely vehicle for a baby. You, for instance, were delivered by a bald eagle. Swooped in here one morning — powerful, elegant, regal. Dropped you on the sofa — a nice, plush fall. Lingered for a while, perched on the kitchen cabinet, while Ellen got things under control. Then he flew away.

"I see you don't believe me. Well, here. Proof: he left a feather."

He did what he could to teach me, of course. To teach me to be like him. We started with some very simple exercises when I was about ten.

"Just take something and make it a little bigger than it is," he said. We were sitting on the front porch. The farm spread out before us. In the distance, we could see one of our brown and white cows, eating grass. "Take that pine tree, for instance. It's a normal-sized tree, right? Now, just say it's so big that we could build a three-story tree house inside it, and still have room for an attic."

I looked at him.

"*Granddaddy,*" I said.

"What? What's the problem?"

"I *can't*," I said. "I mean, I could. But that's just a tree."

"So it is," he said. "Fair enough. Let's try something a little more personal. What do you tell people about your limp?"

"My limp?"

"What do you tell people about that?"

"The truth," I said. "Because my left leg is a little shorter than my right. That I was born that way."

"This is what you tell people?" he said. He looked at me, away from me, back to me again. "Hey, you know, it's your leg," he said. "But if it were mine, I think something more *interesting* might have occurred."

"Like?"

"Like any number of things, depending on who you were talking to. Like, for instance, because you didn't eat your vegetables and this is what happens when you don't — say if you were talking to a little kid — or you had to have some bone removed because you were born without cartilage in your nose. Or you got run over by a train or bitten by an alligator or . . . *something*. I don't know. These are just off the top of my head."

He stopped and straightened up, as though an idea had literally struck him.

"Tell them you're Vulcan's little brother."

"What?"

"You know, Vulcan," he said, pointing north, where we could just see the statue's outstretched hand pointing at the edge of the sky. "Vulcan had a limp too. He was thrown from Mount Olympus one time, for — I can never remember what, exactly. Messing around with somebody. Or maybe it was because he *had* a limp. It doesn't matter. The point is, he was a god, and he was thrown out of heaven, and he had a limp. Like you. So, I don't know. Maybe you can tell people you're related to Vulcan in some way."

"I've got it," I said. "I can tell them Vulcan is my dad." He gave me a look. I think he was a little hurt. But then he smiled.

"Yes," he said, nodding, as if he were considering it, seriously, for the first time. "You're a god. I'd go with that."

"True beauty never lasts long in this world, Thomas. That's why you need to be careful. Don't give yourself to a woman too soon. Because we see what happens, don't we? They will leave you. One way or another they will leave you. Your grandmother, so beautiful, perfect in almost every way: gone. What a companion she was, Thomas. What a passionate companion. And your mother! Oh, what a beauty! Your grandmother's twin, almost: eerie, how alike they were, inside and out. They were the most beautiful women in the world. Your mother was so beautiful, in fact, that when the gods saw her they were jealous, and decided that the only way she could be allowed to live is if she became invisible, and all memory of her loveliness eradicated from the human mind. From all but my own. They left that memory there to curse me. But that's what happened to her. She exists, but she has been made to disappear, and, well, she hasn't been seen since. My fear is that they're coming after Anna next, then you, and all the beauty in the world. Obviously, there's no need to worry about me. I am sufficiently ugly to live a very long time."

Finally, though, inevitably, my grandfather met the man who would be his downfall and mark the end of his career as a professional liar. I was fifteen years old by then and not as present in the household as I used to be. But I know how it happened, or how it must have happened, as I pieced the story together over time. It went like this.

A tall, gaunt-looking man walked into his office one day, holding a briefcase, and, after shaking my grandfather's hand, sat down heavily in a chair, the desk between them.

"Ames," the man said. "Clarence Ames."

"Edmund Rider," he said.

They stared at each other for a moment, and my grandfather wasn't sure at first that Mr. Ames wasn't insane in some way. His hair was uncombed, unwashed, pushed back from his forehead with his fingers, so deeply greased you could tell exactly where the fingers had been. He looked as if he hadn't slept for days, his face was so drawn, his eyes so hooded, and dark, and without expression.

"My wife has died," Mr. Ames said haltingly. He smiled then, but not because he was happy. It was because he didn't know what a smile was anymore, or what one meant. It was just something his face could do, so he did it. Edmund understood this. "This was last week," the man said, "though time has seemed to curl back into itself since then. But it was last week. She was sick for some time. Teresa, her name was. I called her Tess. We came from a small town, Mr. Rider. I've known her all my life. I was with her, of course, every moment I possibly could be. Not that there was anything I could do but make sure she was comfortable . . . but I did that," he said, and smiled again. "I did the best I could."

"I'm sure you did," Edmund said. "I'm sorry, very sorry for your loss. I've lost my wife too."

"Then you know," he said, and Edmund nodded.

"I know," he said. "I know. Grief sometimes takes on a life of its own."

"It's the house, Mr. Rider," he said, "the house that we lived in. I don't want to live there anymore."

Edmund nodded. "Too many memories," he said.

"No," Mr. Ames said, the word almost lifting him out of his chair, so that he seemed to float there for a moment. Then he settled back down. "There can never be enough memories. Isn't that what you discovered? I mean, *I* will never have enough. I've already begun to lose some of them. Things I used to remember,

I don't anymore. I've started writing everything down, though," he said, on a bright note, lifting his briefcase. "They're all in here. Notebook after notebook. I don't sleep much because if I sleep I'm afraid that when I wake more will be lost. Every time I think of something about Tess, no matter how small, I write it down. Who knows if I'll ever think of it again."

"Because as you forget," Edmund said, "she seems to drift farther and farther away. You hold on to what you can, but nothing sustains your grip. Soon even the words just become words."

"Yes," he said.

"I wish I could help," Edmund said.

"You can," Mr. Ames said, this time in a whisper. "My wife is dead, Mr. Rider. We had no children. We . . . couldn't. So she, she was — well, she was everything to me. I would have to say that she was everything to me. We had a lovely house, where we lived together, and where she died. But she's gone from that house forever. I know it. I know it — here," he said, and pointed to his heart. "I'm not crazy. I can tell that's what you're thinking. But I'm not. She lived there, and she died there, and she's never coming back."

Edmund didn't know what to say then — what could he say? — so he just nodded as sympathetically as he could.

The man leaned in a little closer.

"I hear *things* about you, Mr. Rider," the man said. "You sell more than houses, don't you?"

No one had ever said this to my grandfather before, not in the way this man was saying it to him. Where would he have heard such a thing? He looked at Mr. Ames, then away to his realtor's license, which was framed and hanging on the wall behind him.

"Yes," Edmund said. "I sell more than houses."

Mr. Ames leaned in even closer. He smiled, a nearly authentic smile, and Edmund smiled too.

"It's the stories we tell ourselves about ourselves," he said, "that really keep us going. Without them, what do we have?"

"What I want to do," Mr. Ames said, "is buy a house where my wife might come and visit and talk to me, sometime. Something friendly to spirits, and the like. A private place with a garden, possibly, a long driveway, a fireplace, bay windows, a pond. I just want a house where she might feel comfortable coming to visit now and again. Can you possibly help me?"

The man had been leaning ever closer to my grandfather's desk as he spoke, and by the time he finished his face was halfway over the desk itself. My grandfather, meanwhile, was leaning back in his big leather chair, until the headrest was scraping against the wall. Still, their eyes were locked. Neither man blinked. Mr. Ames swallowed again, and breathed, and my grandfather brought his hands together, as though in prayer, and placed them against his chin.

"I know just the place," he said.

It was a cottage near Edgewood, surrounded by oak trees and maple trees. It stood at the end of a long driveway, with bay windows, a working fireplace, a garden growing on the sun side, and a pond out back, full of orange and black koi. The two men walked the property together. It was a warm spring day. A wind came up and caught the branches of a small dogwood, and the tree gently swayed. The rooms inside were bright, but old. The ceiling plaster had fallen in places, revealing crossbeams. The hardwood floor buckled and dipped, and the closets were small and dark.

"An old couple used to live here," my grandfather said. "They lived here for twenty, thirty years. They did everything together, people tell me. Walked together, same time every day. Worked in the garden together. When one of them sneezed, the other one caught a cold."

He laughed a little, glanced at Mr. Ames.

"As they grew older, their biggest concern was which of the two of them would be the first to die. The other didn't know if he — she — could go on alone. Of course, deep down they both assumed that they would die at the same moment, that because they did everything else together, like Siamese twins or something, they would both go nearly simultaneously. But that isn't what happened.

"She died first. He grieved, and waited for death. Every night he prayed that this would be his last. But the nights began to add up. Weeks, months went by, and still he lived. He walked, gardened, slept alone, and waited for death. He lived another ten years. Extraordinary years, though, his neighbors tell me, full of wonder and surprise. He even met someone — not wife material, but a woman with whom he could share his days."

He paused. (This was the professional pause, the expert kind of pause that marked the difference between seeming sincerity and unctuous hucksterism.)

"This has been a difficult house to sell. It's old and falling apart. They're thinking of putting a mall in one street over. And the thing is, people say it's haunted. That the two of them, once they were together again, never really left. People hear things, see things. I don't know, Mr. Ames. Some people don't want to see ghosts. Others do. You might be happy here."

"Not happy," Mr. Ames said, looking around him as though he were seeing things already. "I don't intend to be happy. But you know, I think I sense something already."

"I'll leave you alone," my grandfather said, and on that note, it was a sale, and he came home that night beaming.

He had the occasion to drive past Mr. Ames's new house once or twice over the next few weeks, sometimes with me in the car with him, and he would tell me this story over and over, how with his own words he had made a new world for this old man, and though he couldn't see the house from the road he often slowed to gaze at the wall of surrounding maples and oak trees, his fingers literally crossed. He never stopped. He rarely visited with the people he sold his houses to, afraid that his presence might break whatever spell the house and its occupants were under.

But one day driving through Edgewood we actually saw Mr. Ames, at the very end of his driveway, coming for his mail. This was a good sign, my grandfather said. To be looking for mail indicated expectation, anticipation — possibly even faith in an unknown future, and other signs of life. "I remember the first time I checked the mail," he said, "after." My grandfather slowed, honked his horn to wave. Mr. Ames opened the mailbox, and both of them saw the same thing at the same time: nothing. Not a flyer, not even a *To Whom It May Concern.* At that moment my grandfather could imagine nothing sadder than a widower peering into an empty mailbox. He said as much to me. It was then that the sound of the horn seemed to reach him, and Mr. Ames looked up. My grandfather forced a smile and waved. But Mr. Ames didn't recognize him, or perhaps he couldn't see him through the windshield, and so he didn't wave back. He just watched us drive by, his face blank, unmoved, turning as the car passed, hands at his side. We saw him framed in the rearview mirror, growing smaller and smaller. Mr. Ames looked even paler now, if possible, my grandfather said, even thinner and more hollowed out than he had before. He looked like a man who had not seen a ghost.

"She ran away seventeen times. The first time she ran away she was three. She made it to Georgia. The second time she was seven, and I thought I'd never find her, but she left a paper trail. The next fourteen times I just hoped and prayed she'd come back, and she always did, until the very last, the seventeenth time. She was kind of a wildcat, your mother. She liked the open road, a sense of mystery — like me. We had a special connection. We read the same books at the same time. I bought paperbacks so after I'd finished reading the first part I could just tear off a hunk and hand it to her. But after her mother died everything changed. I don't — can't — blame her. It wasn't just her. It was as if we didn't speak the same language anymore. Literally. I could not understand the words coming out of her mouth, and she couldn't understand mine. So she left. She went away and she never came back. And that was the seventeenth time."

Three months later, my grandfather was asked to come by the offices of the Realtor's Association for a visit with the president. It was in the afternoon, after school, and so he took me with him. He knew the president, Avery Merrill, extremely well; he was the man who gave my grandfather his award every year, and they played golf together. My grandfather assumed it was something along these lines that Avery wanted to discuss with him, or perhaps to make him aware of some new award he was up for.

We stopped by the little glass building where the Realtor's Association was housed. Avery Merrill, a short, thin man with an oversize brown mustache, was on the telephone when we arrived, and he gestured my grandfather into his office, pointing to a chair, winking, waving to me, all the while saying, "I see, sure, I'll talk to the bank and get back to you." After he got off the phone he said, "Money!" and rolled his eyes. He shook my grandfather's hand and they both sat down.

"It's good to see you, Edmund," he said. "You too, Thomas. How's life treating you?"

And then, without waiting for an answer, he leaned over and whispered in my grandfather's ear, just loud enough for me to hear, "You might not should have brought him."

"Oh?"

"We have some . . . serious issues to discuss."

"I see," he said, considering what Avery had said. "Well, Thomas can hear anything you have to tell me. Right, kiddo? He's fifteen now, nearly a man. What's the problem?"

"The problem," he said, and he glanced down at some paper that was on his desk and sighed. "Okay. Do you remember — let's see, where's the name? — here — Clarence Ames? You sold him a two-bedroom in Edgewood some time back."

"Of course," my grandfather said. "I remember Mr. Ames."

"Okay. And did you happen to mention to him, in the course of selling him the house, that somehow he might end up being able to visit with his wife" — he looked over at me, not sure whether he wanted me to hear the next part — "who was dead?"

"I don't know if I actually *said* that," Edmund said, thinking back. "I may have suggested it."

"You may have *suggested* it," Avery said. This clearly made no sense to him. "I'm not sure I follow you. Did you imply something about him and his wife? I mean, she was — she was dead, Edmund. Still is, as far as I know."

"He was grief-stricken," my grandfather said. "This is something I happen to understand. The house I sold him, I thought it was a good place for a man like that."

"Well, he wants his money back."

"His money back?"

"And he's willing to sue for it. You, me, the Realtor's Association. Everybody. That and damages."

"What damages?"

"*Emotional* damages. He's a lawyer. He says he hasn't seen his wife in the three months he's lived there, and he says that was the basis for the sale. He also says, though I find this even harder to believe, that you encouraged him to kill himself."

"I *what*?"

"Some story you told about an old couple . . . one dying and one not and them not being able to be together until they both died or some such thing. Honestly, he lost me."

"That wasn't my *point*," my grandfather said. He rolled his eyes, and I rolled mine, but for completely different reasons.

"My point was that he had a lot of life left in him. That he could live without her. It was so obvious. I can't believe he missed it."

Avery stared at him, uncomprehending. My grandfather looked to me for help, but I couldn't give him any. Avery was saying only what I had already said a hundred times.

"But what does that have to do with the *house,* Edmund?"

My grandfather smiled and shook his head.

"I've never sold a house in my life," my grandfather said. "I don't know anything about houses."

Avery cocked his head to one side, staring at my grandfather.

"You know, I've always admired your way with words," Avery said. "Your . . . imagination. It's what makes you special. It's what makes you the best. For my money, anyway, you're the best. But you're a *realtor,* Edmund. You're not a shrink. Or a doctor. You're not anything."

My grandfather looked at me. He wished I wasn't there to hear that, I could see it in his eyes, and I wished the same thing. I didn't want to see him this way. And I wanted to say something. I thought I should be defending him, but no words came. What could I say, after all? Avery was right. My grandfather wasn't anything but a collection of stories he'd made up about himself and the world. He may have been happier living in that world, but I wasn't, and neither was Avery Merrill. I felt the blood rush to my face, and I turned away. He was on his own.

"I know what I am, Avery," he said, his voice taking on a steely edge. "I don't need you to tell me what I am and what I'm not."

Avery touched the papers on his desk. I could tell he was about to get angry himself, but didn't because I was there.

"You doing all right, Thomas?" he said.

"Sure," I said. "I'm fine."

"Because you can go get a cola if you want to. There's a machine —"

"He can hear this," my grandfather said. "He's already heard that I'm nothing, according to you. How much worse can it be?"

Avery nodded.

"I was just going to say," he said, "that this isn't the first time someone's complained."

"Oh?" he said.

"No," Avery said. "Hardly." He consulted his notes again. "This is just the first time I thought it might become a problem."

"Who?" my grandfather demanded. "What? I want to know."

"And I'm going to tell you," he said. "There was that fellow, that investment banker, who had quit his job to write a book. And you told him that the house he was looking at, I think you said something like Edgar Allan Poe had lived there for a few months while he was composing 'The Raven.' With a cousin, was it? You showed him the room where he slept. Told him the poem had originally been called 'The Jackal' or the 'The Vulture.' He eventually found out this wasn't true and was quite upset. Writer's block ensued. He went back into investment banking."

"I'm sorry about that," Edmund said. "But he seemed perfectly happy to believe me at the time. He said it was 'inspiring.'"

"And here's one that's somewhat unclear to me. Did you suggest to a woman suffering from arthritis that there was a large vein of nickel running beneath the foundation of her house — nickel, which you said in laboratory tests has put rats with arthritis into remission? Do rats even get arthritis? Edmund?"

"The placebo effect," he said. "Sometimes it's as powerful as a drug."

"My personal favorite," Avery said, "is the house on Mayfair

Drive. Apparently, not only has a herd of monarch butterflies *not* descended upon their home, but they can't even get a bird to eat at their feeder."

"I can't explain about the birds," he said. "I have *no* idea about the birds. But I told them that when you flushed the toilet in the basement the upstairs shower went hot. I didn't have to, but I did. They bought the home anyway."

"You've been misleading people, Edmund," Avery said in a softer, but darker, voice.

"Not *misleading*," he said. "I wouldn't say misleading."

"Actually, I was trying to be gentle," Avery said. "You've been lying."

My grandfather nodded. "I suppose I have," he said. He cut his eyes at me and laughed. "But what's so bad about that? I wish someone would tell *me* a story sometimes. One I could believe in. Other than the one I have. You know, it wasn't this way when Ellen was alive. I was happy with the way things were. Unbelievably so."

Avery nodded.

"I realize you've had a tough go of it, Edmund," he said, rubbing the tip of his thumb back and forth against his fingers. "Ellen, and then Lucy. I don't know how well I would have done under the same circumstances."

"And you don't know the half of it," Edmund said wearily.

Avery, who had known my grandfather for twenty years, cocked his head. "I don't?"

"I'm also a fugitive," he said.

Avery glanced at me, and I looked at Edmund. I couldn't believe he was doing this, now.

"Oh. Really?" Avery said, wearily. I could see he had given up. So had I. But this didn't stop my grandfather.

"That's right. I killed a man," he said matter-of-factly. He glanced over at me, caught my eye. "I should have told you this,

Thomas — I had planned to, but it never came up. Now it has and you know. I killed a man, a long time ago. It was an accident, but I had to leave the little town I came from. I never went back. I changed my name, my entire identity. Then, when I met Ellen, I thought that was all over. The lying, I mean. It's been a huge burden for me to carry around with me all these years. And I think, I think it's what's led to all these . . . other things. My wife, Lucy. Et cetera. It's payback, Avery. What goes around, comes around. This is a proven, scientific fact."

But Avery had stopped listening. He had heard enough of my grandfather's stories for one day. Me, I'd heard enough for my entire life.

"Well," Avery said, ending the meeting with a sigh, "as you must know, these are ethical violations. You're my friend, and this is very difficult for me. But we can't afford to be sued. Your actions reflect on us all. I'm going to have to take this up before the board, Edmund. And I'll be very surprised if your license is not revoked."

My grandfather nodded and smiled. "I'll be surprised as well," he said.

It was a long drive home. We were quiet the way people are when they have a lot to say but they don't know how to say it. That, or they don't want to. I didn't even look at him. I couldn't. I stared out my window and leaned against the door, creating as much distance between us as possible.

"I remember when this was all just woods," he said, indicating with a hand all the fast-food joints and malls on both sides of the road. I felt him look at me. I pushed my hair out of my eyes and didn't say a word. "When you were born," he said, "there was just this one road. And nothing anywhere but pine trees."

"When I was born," I said.

"That's right," he said, and I knew I shouldn't have said it, because that got him to thinking. "When you were born — I wouldn't say *born,* exactly. I guess *appeared* is more like it. When you appeared —"

"Jesus," I said, under my breath.

"What?"

His foot, reflexively, hit the brake. I shook my head.

"Nothing," I said.

A car behind us honked, and my grandfather stepped on the gas a little. But he was a slow driver. Everybody passed us. There was another mall going up in a broken field to the right, and even I could remember when that was all just woods. It was just last week.

"I'm sorry," he said. "About what happened back there. It kind of came out of left field. Had I known, I wouldn't have brought you. You shouldn't have to hear people say that kind of thing about your grandfather."

I looked at him. And I couldn't help it: I laughed.

"Shouldn't have to *hear* it?" I said. "What else have I been hearing all my life? Stories. Lies. Made-up crap. Excuse my French. But Zeus, Ares, *storks* — it's crap. I was born like anybody else is born, and then my mother died."

"Obviously," he said.

"Then why don't you just *say* that?" I said.

"Okay," he said. "Okay. You were born like anybody else, and then your mother died."

It was the first time in my life he had spoken plainly. This was a beginning. Just hearing that, that *fact,* made me feel more substantial.

He drove on, cars zooming past us on either side.

"Okay. And then?" I said. "Or — before? What happened before?"

"Well, now *that's* another story," he said.

"Another story," I said, giving up all hope. "Great. All I need is another story." I turned away and watched the roadside construction crews directing traffic through an intersection. I wanted to jump out.

"Hey, don't worry," he said. He reached across the seat between us and held my knee. He did this to show affection sometimes. "It's all going to be fine. *You're* going to be fine. The problem, Thomas, is everybody else. Other people . . . people like Avery, Mr. Ames . . . they're not open. There is so much for them in the world and yet they refuse to see it. You know why? Because they're small-minded. And do you know why they're small-minded? Because they come from small towns. Seriously. Think about it. This is true. Everybody talks about the big cities, but the world is made up mostly of small towns, and people from small towns have small minds, small hearts, and a small vision. Most of them, anyway. There are exceptions. Some of the ones who get out are okay, but for most, there's just no hope for them. This is why I think you're going to be a special person, Thomas. One reason, anyway. You're not from a small town. You're a very matter-of-fact young man now, but I see that changing down the line. Because not only are you *not* from a small town, you're really not from anywhere at all. The television you watch, the music you listen to, the books you read — you could be from anywhere. *And that's good.* I would never say this to anybody but you; it would give them the wrong impression. But you're better than they are, Thomas. You're better than the small-town people. They have a past; that's the thing, and that's what holds them back. It's like a wall they can't get over or around. Whereas you, all you have is the wide-open blue of the future. Keep it that way. Keep your eyes on what's ahead. You're young. Don't worry about what's happened already, and if somebody tries to tell you different, just say — what is it you say? *'Whatever'* — and go on with your life. Don't become like them, Thomas."

I looked out the window. I would have liked a past. But I didn't tell him this.

"Whatever," I said.

It was a quiet ride home.

"A year after you were born," he told me, "before the main highway even came out so far and later became overrun with gas stations, super malls, and fast-food restaurants, I went on a long country drive and found the ten acres where we eventually ended up living for sale. Anna and I still lived in Edgewood, in the house filled with memories of Ellen and Lucy, and we were thinking of buying our first home together, far away from the past. The property was completely undeveloped, but I saw what I thought it could become and fell in love with that vision, and we left you with a sitter and I brought Anna out to look at it. She was open to looking at anything, she always said. So we walked the perimeter. I showed her where the driveway would go, and the house, and where we would sit in the evening watching the night come on. It was very nice, she said, all of it, the trees and the quiet, and the lovely view. She especially liked the deer tracks through the woods — reindeer, I said. But she wasn't really sure she wanted to live so far out. After leaving Ashland, she had come to like big-city life.

"'It took us almost twenty minutes to get out here,' she said, kicking the straw-covered dirt with her toe.

"'You are standing in your living room,' I said, though she was leaning against a pine tree. 'Think about it, Anna, your own living room!'

"'And where are you?'

"'I'm in the kitchen,' I said.

"'Could you get me something to drink then?' she asked me. 'I'm thirsty.'

"I laughed a little, and so did she, then she walked over to me and draped her arms around my neck and hugged me.

"'It's just so far into town,' she said into my ear.

"'The town will be here soon enough,' I said, 'and then you'll only wish it could be farther.'

"I pushed her away from me and looked into her eyes. Then I turned her so that she could see the outstretched hand of Vulcan, on Red Mountain, so many miles away. The sun was setting, blazing above the edge of the hills. I walked away from her suddenly, and then with my arms gestured to the entire expanse before us.

"'Don't you realize where we are, Anna?' I said. 'Do you have any idea? Why this place instead of some other, in town or down the road? Because when Vulcan was kicked out of Mount Olympus, this is where he fell! On this very mountain. This is where all the gods fall, in and around this very spot. Who knows that we might not wake up in the morning and see one, hobbling down the driveway? How can we possibly pass that up?'"

The worst kind of trouble a self-made man can get into is when he doesn't know what to make of himself anymore. This is exactly what happened to my grandfather. With the revocation of his realtor's license, he changed. He didn't do much talking or pay much attention to either of us. It was weird. I felt preorphaned — orphaned before the fact. It was a lonely time for everybody. He moved around the house aimlessly, as though looking for some lost thing, and it wasn't me or Anna, though we were lost as much as he was now. Ostensibly to go on errands, he and I would drive around town, slowing past houses with FOR SALE signs stuck in the yard, and he would mumble something about square footage, and abutments, and falling stars. It was the beginning of a decline that lasted three years. He eventually became a much quieter man — and a smaller one too. Because he was not made out of flesh and blood: he was made up mostly of stories, a high-wire act of a life balanced on the suspension of disbelief, and as he became deprived of his stories he actually seemed to shrink. He missed my high school graduation and slept through my eighteenth birthday. That last Christmas we walked over to see Mrs. Nevins, who it seemed would live forever, and she gave him the lucky dime, instead of me.

"He needs it more," she said.

But I was right about that dime stuff all along. There was nothing to it.

A week later he was dead.

It was a warm winter day when we brought his ashes back home and spread them, according to his instructions, "here and there across the fields of his domain." Ellen was out here, somewhere, too. He had saved her ashes in an urn until he settled down, and alone one night he had taken a walk and done what we were doing then. It was kind of weird and kind of exhilarating at the same time. The cows watched us, this man and woman carefully stepping around their shit, trying to spread Edmund Rider as evenly as we could, here and there across the fields. Anna and I actually laughed when the wind blew some of the ashes that she had thrown high into the air back in our faces and in our eyes. We laughed, but it was too much for me. I started crying — from laughter straight to tears. I told her it was the ashes in my eyes, but she knew better. She took my hand and held it hard. I tried to stop crying, but the more I tried, the worse it got, because it had come to me then as a hard truth that now I really *was* orphaned, and it was the truest, deepest, and purest feeling of being alone in the world that I could ever imagine. I would always have Anna, of course, but it's not enough in this world to have people who just love you. You have to share the same blood. And who *was* she, anyway? After all these years, I didn't really know. So I looked at her, and she looked at me, and, standing out there in the middle of that pine-infested farm, with my grandfather in my eyes, I asked her.

"Who *are* you?" I said.

And this, without hesitation, is what she said to me: "Thomas," she said, "I was your mother's last, best friend."

And somehow, this made me smile.

"Sounds like there's a story there," I said.

"There is," she said. "There is. Listen."

And I did.

THREE

*T*he town emerged a few miles past the freeway exit, its rooftops and church spires just visible above a long, thick stand of pine like some forgotten land, heretofore beyond the ken of us all. An old cinder-block gas station sat forsaken at the city limits, its ancient pumps rusted brown. It all looked like the dead and dried-out bones of some primitive animal. The forest, which had been cleared for construction however many years ago, now seemed bent on reclaiming what it had lost: grass grew in patches through the cracked concrete, and summer vines, a kind of ivy, swirled everywhere around it. This is where I stopped.

I tried to imagine my mother stopping here on her first day, reluctant to go any farther. She had that hair, those eyes, that smile. How far can this possibly take me? *Here, just an hour and a half away from home, this is what she may have been thinking. She pulled up to the pumps, waiting for something. When some grease monkey in an oil-stained jumpsuit finally walked out to greet her, she remembered what it was she needed.* "Fill her up," *she said.* "Please."

"Yes ma'am."

"And — is there a ladies' room?"

"'Round back," he said, and he watched her walk the entire way, until she disappeared behind the station.

I called Anna and told her where I was. She was pleased. After a moment she said, "I guess you should head on into town."

"I guess I should," *I said.*

But I didn't move. A car drove by then, rusted in spots, spewing fumes from the exhaust. It slowed when it saw me, a stranger in a phone booth on the outskirts of town. It almost stopped, and as it did I could make out an old man inside it. He waved at me as if he knew me, and I waved back, and his lips curled. Then he drove away.

I said, "This is hard."

"It is," she said. "I know it is."

"I don't know what I'm doing."

"Just talk to people," she said. "That's all you have to do. Say your mother's name, once, and believe me, people will talk. It's what they do best."

"I'll pretend I'm a detective or something."

"Exactly," she said, and laughed. "A detective."

"But what if they act all weird and stuff and I want to go?"

"Then —"

And she said something else, but the line went dead. I didn't call her back. Instead, I walked behind the station to the men's room, and though the toilet here was dry and dark and had been for who knows how many years, I used it. Force of habit. I think I drowned a spider. The vines back here had grown through the doorway, through the broken windows, and were embracing every brick, taking over everything, growing with a relentless kind of manifest destiny, over, around, and through whatever was in their way. I thought if I stared at them long enough, I could probably see them move. And I did watch them for a while, alone behind that building, unable or unwilling to go a step farther.

If she could do it, I thought, so could I. I got in my car and followed the ghost of my mother up the hill and into the town.

I drove up the hill and into town. I would talk to people about my mother later; I'd spend three days talking about my mother. But now it was just me, looking around. And I don't know what I expected, but there was almost nothing there. A few stores on two city blocks. Some dark, others with big GOING OUT OF BUSINESS signs on them. I drove through the town and it was gone in a blink. I turned right at the railroad trestle, because the railroad trestle was still there — Anna said she thought it would be — and I headed straight to the Hargraves place. Two rights and a left. And there it was in front of me, glorious and decrepit. My inheritance.

The place was a wreck, completely uninhabitable. Kudzu scaled the outside walls and weedy vines slithered through the broken windows. Shrubs had grown shaggy and huge, and a tree had fallen into the screen porch on the side of the house, ripping off half its roof. And yet the lawn was nicely mowed; even the edges by the sidewalk had been trimmed. Inside the house you could hear the little feet of the animals who had taken possession of the place, the squirrels and mice, scurrying into the walls, the flutter of wings. I felt like an intruder there. In the living room, three old chairs sat in a circle around a puddle of candle wax and cigarette butts. I imagined a group of high school kids coming here on the weekends, the kind of kids I never knew that well, smoking and drinking. It was a thrill for them, I bet, being in a place where someone had died. I walked upstairs to the bedroom. There was a mattress, heavy on the floor; this is probably where they came to make out. And more. I'd done that before myself, of course, found a quiet, dark place to go with a girl and kiss her, to hold her close as she held me, until it felt like only a minor membrane kept our beating hearts apart.

The air was thick and hot, like an attic, almost too thick to breathe. My shirt was soaked in sweat. I unbuttoned it and looked around. Stacked against one wall was a pyramid of beer cans; written across another above an old dresser in a Magic Marker's scrawl: LUCY HARGRAVES WAS HERE. Hargraves? Her story had gotten confused with that of the man who came before her, but this was the way ghost stories got told, I guess; over time the ghosts themselves got mixed up. Memory fades when people disappear, and they never come back to set you straight. A patch of old sunlight fell through the window and across the hardwood floor. A shadow that wasn't a shadow spread along the edge of the mattress. I knelt down and pushed the mattress aside. And there, across the floorboards, this dark stain. Blood? Possibly. Maybe something else. But say it was blood, eighteen years old. Then this would be the room where I was born. Here I'd been and here I was again, the room in the house in the town where all of it had happened, just as Anna said it had. Closing my eyes I could see it: my dying mother, Anna, and the crowd outside, waiting for their king. If all that could have possibly happened.

I walked to the dresser and opened a drawer: empty. But in the next drawer, a piece of paper, handwritten words filling one whole side. I sat back on the mattress and read:

Yea it is said unto you that a child will be born, and that this child will be a boy. You will have known much affliction before he comes, and often, but true misery will follow in his wake.

How will we know this child?

He will have no father, and no mother, and not even know his own name. Though dead to you, yet he shall live.

What will become of the boy?

He will leave you and take everything that is yours with him. Your fields will bake beneath the unforgiving sun, and nothing there will grow.

Then what will become of us?

The hard times will make you stronger, and your patience will bring with it a prize. For one day the true king shall return, dragging a leg behind him, and he will come to the elders and ask them for help, for he is young and he knows not who he is.

And he will be chosen?

Though known to all he will still be chosen. And yea, though there is no greater honor, the king himself may be the last to know it in his heart. Thus until the festival itself and the ceremony of the seed he should be watched by every eye in the village and not allowed to wander far. He should be made handsome to look at, and before he is crowned all the women should see him, for when the sun sets one of them shall have him. And then he will take the least likely among you, and he will plant his seed within her. Thus he will herald a new beginning. The crops will grow plentiful again, and you will reclaim your place in the world.

And until then, what shall we do?

Tell this story.

I had a sick feeling inside. I couldn't breathe. What was this? Anna hadn't mentioned anything about this. I had to get out. I ran down the stairs and over the lawn and got into my car and drove back into town, where I stopped. The streets were empty. I caught my breath. Finally I saw an old man sitting on a bench below an awning, and I asked him if he knew of a place I could stay for a few days, and he told me, among other things that I wrote down later, about Mrs. Parsons, whose house was only a

151

few blocks away. Everything in Ashland was only a few blocks away. Not even a thousand people lived there. The town was quiet in an eerie way, and still, as though it were two-dimensional, in black and white, and I was the only real and colorful thing in it. I wasn't, though; there were other colorful things.

I drove to Mrs. Parsons's house and knocked. A minute passed and I knocked again. An old lady opened the door, and she looked at me and her eyes grew wide, and she smiled.

"My," she said, full of wonder, surprise. "Aren't you a beautiful young man."

"Oh," I said, blushing. No one had ever said such a thing to me before. "Thank you. I guess?"

"Handsome, I should say," she said, still staring. "Men don't like to be called beautiful, even when they are. I understand. I shouldn't have said a thing. But at my age I can get away with it. It's one of the privileges. Would you like to come in?"

"Yes," I said. "Thank you. I —"

"You'd be wanting a room, wouldn't you?" she said as we walked into the dark entrance hall. The walls were wood paneled. The knotholes looked like a monster's eyes.

"Yes," I said. "Please. I'm just here for a little while. I've come because —"

"Lucy!" she called out.

How did she know? I felt my heart rattle against my chest, as I heard the rapid approach of footsteps from another room. I thought, *So she isn't dead. Is that what this is all about? Is this what Anna thought I would find? That she's lived here, in this house, for the last eighteen years?* I could believe this for an instant, the same way I'd believed I'd seen Edmund driving a car, three days after he died, and I'd had to accelerate beside the car and stare to prove to myself it wasn't him.

"Lucy," she said again as the face of a young black woman peered around a doorway. She looked at us with the startled eyes of a doe. Her hair was short and black, cropped close to her skull, which was perfectly round. Her lips were a deep orange. Her skin was the color of a dried leaf but as smooth as water. And she was young, my age or thereabouts. "A fine specimen of man we have here, do we not? Is he beautiful? Or would you call him merely handsome? Better to be beautiful, I think."

"Mrs. Parsons," she said quietly, smiling, looking away from us to the floor. But I got the feeling she thought I was. I thought she was, in the brief moment I had to look at her. I couldn't take all of her in, she was so pretty. I spent too much time on each part of her: her eyes, her lips, her shoulders, and all the way down.

"I think we need to dust the room," Mrs. Parsons said, "before we allow him to see it. Unless he doesn't mind dust. Or even prefers it. People come in all shapes and sizes. I imagine there are some who actually *like* dust."

"I don't mind it," I said.

"Go ahead anyway, Lucy," she said. "Take a rag to it, why don't you."

"Yes ma'am," she said.

Mrs. Parsons shook her head and gazed at her.

"Why do you always call me 'ma'am' when people are about? She never does when we're alone," she said to me in a confidential tone. "She's the one telling *me* what to do." Mrs. Parsons laughed, and Lucy, blushing, nodded once at me and quickly took the stairs.

"She is my arms and my legs and most of my brain," she said. "And a pleasure just to look at. Like you. That's the main reason she's here, honestly: to remind me what's it like to be young and lovely. Come in. Sit down. Let me look at *you*."

We sat in her dusty living room, the window blinds shut against the light.

"So," she said. "Where you from?"

"Birmingham," I said.

"Birmingham," she said, as though the word itself conjured an amazing and mystical place in her head. "I had an aunt who visited Birmingham once."

"Really?"

"Got lost," she said.

"Really?"

"It's like a maze," she said.

"Birmingham?"

"Everything," she said. "A wonderful, complex, never-ending maze. Thirsty? When Lucy comes back down she'll bring us something."

"I'm fine," I said. "Thank you."

"You know what? I am too," she said. "All things being equal. I mean, I *could* complain, but it's not in my nature. I like to keep a smile on my face even when things are falling *completely* apart. And things always seem to be falling apart, don't they? Just so slowly sometimes it's hard to notice."

"Well —"

"I'm a widow," she said, by way of explanation. "And that's pretty much it. It's like a job now. For an old woman, see, it's not who you are that's so important, but what you've lost. That's the lesson here."

"I'm sorry," I said.

But she brushed my words aside with her hand.

"Oh, well, it happens. Tom died quite some time ago. In his sleep. Breathing one moment, then the next . . . not. On the one hand, I was thankful: dying in your sleep is a blessed thing. On the other, I didn't much like waking up beside a dead person. You know."

"I can imagine," I said.

"Best *not* imagine that," she said, and pointed to her head. "Might get nightmares. I had them for years. The kind where you wake up beside a dead person. Only in the dream it was never Tom. It was always someone famous, like Chuck Heston or Fidel Castro." She laughed. "Sometimes," she said, "I feel completely insane."

"Not really," I said.

"No, I do," she said, smiling brightly. "Completely."

"You said his name was Tom?" I said after a moment. "Your husband's name was Tom? That's funny — interesting, I mean — because that's my name too."

"Really?" she said. "How totally fascinating."

"I go by Thomas, though," I said. "Thomas Rider."

"Well isn't that something?" she said, smiling. You could tell that this warmed her up considerably toward me. "Thomas is a good, strong name. And Rider — that rings a bell, somehow. Do I know your family?"

"You might," I said. "I don't know. My mother — I think my mother lived here for a while, a long time ago. Her name was Rider too. Lucy Rider?"

She nodded, the smile frozen on her face. Then she looked at me, her head slightly cocked to one side, her eyes clear and wide as if I were coming into focus for the first time. It was as if she suddenly recognized me, an old friend from many years ago, or a cousin she'd forgotten she had, or an aunt she'd finally found.

"*Your* mother?" she said, whispering. "Lucy Rider was your *mother*?"

And this is where it started.

"Did you know her?" I said. "Because that's why I'm here."

"Why?"

"To see," I said.

"To see?"

"The truth," I said. "About her. And about what happened to me. I want —"

"A history," she said. "A past. Because if you don't know where you've been, you don't know where you're going."

"Yes," I said. "Did you know her?"

I smiled, and waited, but she didn't seem to be listening anymore. Her eyes were locked on me but strangely vacant, her face and her body still. "Mrs. Parsons?" I said. For a moment I was afraid she had died herself, not in her sleep, like her husband, but midsentence. But then her eyes blinked, once, like a shutter. "Mrs. Parsons?"

"I know your birthday," she said softly.

"I'm sorry?"

"I remember the day you were born," she said. "It was the twenty-fourth of December, nineteen eighty-two. Isn't that right? You must be eighteen. It's been that long, hasn't it, since you've been gone."

"Gone?" I said. "You mean —"

"Born," she said. "I meant born." She had yet to take her eyes off of me, as if she felt that if she looked away I might not be there when she looked back again. "It's hard to tell. How much you know, how much you understand. But you'll understand everything soon enough," she said. "We'll all understand, in time. I think that's the lesson here. Now, stay right where you are, please. I must tell the others you're here."

She stood and walked slowly out of the room, backwards, smiling, watching me until she turned the corner, where I heard her pick up the phone and dial.

"Carlton?" I heard her say. "Emma Parsons. He's back, Carlton. The boy, he's *back.*"

She was quiet, listening to him. "Fine," she said. "Okay. Yes. Of course." Then she hung up the phone and looked at me.

"Some people will be coming by in just a minute," she said. "To say hello. Welcome you to Ashland. Kind of like from the chamber of commerce, the welcome wagon. You know."

"Okay," I said. "Maybe they'll know something about my mother too."

"Maybe they will," she said, nodding. "I wouldn't be surprised if they do."

Not long after Mrs. Parsons had made her call, there was a knock on the front door, and this time Lucy went to answer it. I peered after her. Her hand on the doorknob, she turned to look at me too and sort of rolled her eyes. "Lucy," a man said, nodding as he and two other men walked past her. She closed the door and disappeared into a back room. Mrs. Parsons stood and met the three men at the door to the sitting room.

"Carlton," she said. "How nice of you to come. Al," she said. "Welcome. And Sugar," she said. "Did you wipe your feet, Sugar? Thank you. Come in, please. This way."

She led them to the living room like a museum guide, slowing before me, the exhibit, standing to one side so they all could get a good view.

"Gentlemen," she said. "This here is Thomas Rider. I think you know who he is. Thomas, this is Carlton Snipes, Al Speegle, and — Sugar? Sugar, I don't know your last name. Do you even have one?"

"Sugar is fine," he said, and I stood and shook his hand and each of their hands in turn. I had to match their names against the list of characters I had in my head from the story Anna told me, and they matched up well. I shook Mr. Snipes's hand last, and he held on to it the longest, staring hard and deep into my eyes. He was the evil one. The others, according to Anna, had merely lost their way.

They looked like the Ashland version of the Three Stooges. Snipes was small, all points and edges, even his ears; his eyes were harsh and unflinching. Sugar was fat and dull; he reminded me, somehow, of an amoeba, an amoeba with tobacco stains on its fingers. And Mr. Speegle was a tall man with a stoop and an uncertain way of smiling, as though he wasn't sure a smile was appropriate and didn't want to offend you, so he withdrew the smile, then reintroduced it, over and over again. He wore thick glasses, and his eyes looked kind but distant behind them.

"He — he looks like her," Mr. Speegle said softly, almost as though I weren't there, or as if I couldn't understand his language. "The eyes. She had the same green eyes, didn't she?"

"*Al,*" Carlton Snipes said. But Al wasn't listening.

"And something else. The cheeks, just the way his face — you know, the way it glows. It's like looking at a ghost."

"Al's in love," Sugar said, and laughed. Finally, Mr. Snipes shot a look at him.

"This is not why we're here," Mr. Snipes said sharply. "Of course, he *would* look like his mother. She was — she had a number of strong, attractive qualities. But who else do we see in his face? Al, Sugar? Who do we see there?"

The three of them stared at me together, as one, a kind of three-headed, six-eyed monster picking over my face with its gaze.

"What are you doing?" I said. "Why are you looking at me like that?"

"Not Iggy," Sugar said after staring at me for another moment. "I don't see Iggy there at all."

"Neither do I," Al said.

"Hello," I said.

"Maybe some in the hair," Sugar said. "Iggy's got good hair. You can't deny that."

"Let's concentrate on the face," Snipes said sharply.

"I am," Sugar said. "And I don't see Iggy."

"He's just not there," Al said.

"Iggy," I said, and they looked at me all at once, again, Snipes holding his gaze the longest.

"Do you realize how long that little fucker has been lying to us?" Sugar said. "Nineteen years! That is one long time to keep a lie going. I bet he never even touched her. You know what I'm saying? He's just been holding on to that lie all this time."

"He has a limp," Mrs. Parsons said. She had retreated into the background during their investigation, but she moved forward slightly to inject her offering.

"A limp?" Al said.

"I noticed that first thing," she said, "because of, well, you know. It's a little one. But it's a limp. A definite limp."

"Iggy has a limp," Sugar said, looking at my legs, then over to Snipes and Mr. Speegle.

"Walk around some, Thomas," Mrs. Parsons said sweetly. "So they can see."

"What?"

"Show them how you walk."

"You're kidding."

"Just a little," Mrs. Parsons said.

"Just walk around?" I said.

"Sure," she said and smiled warmly at me. "In a little circle. Right here. So everyone can see."

"Okay," I said, sighing, and I walked around in a circle so that everyone could see the way in which I was uneven, like a wobbly table or chair, always leaning to one side. Anna always called me a sweet boy, by which she meant that I rarely said no to anybody. Asked to walk around in a circle, I did it, a little afraid not to, to see where no would take me.

"That's a limp," Al said, nodding. "That's a limp if I've ever seen one."

Sugar said he thought so too.

"So, how long have you had this *limp*?" Snipes asked me, as though perhaps it was something I had just fabricated for the occasion.

"Since I was born," I said. "One leg is a little shorter than the other one."

Snipes looked hard at me and shook his head.

"So it *could* be Iggy," Sugar said.

"I suppose it's possible," Snipes said.

"Maybe it is him and he didn't go to the face at all but went to the leg instead. That's the kind of fucked-up thing Iggy might do."

"You can watch your language, Sugar," Snipes said.

Sugar breathed in deeply through his nose and shook his head. "I'm only saying," he said, and Mr. Speegle nodded and patted him softly on the back.

"Listen," I said.

Everybody stopped talking and looked at me. But I couldn't continue. I didn't know what else I could say. It was as if the language I brought with me was insufficient. We were not going to understand one another like that, with words. I was just going to have to be there, among them, and see what happened. I shook my head.

"Let's all sit down, why don't we," Mrs. Parsons said brightly. "No law against that, is there? Please. And how would everyone like a glass of sweet tea?"

"If it wouldn't be any trouble," Mr. Speegle said.

"No trouble at all," she said. "Lucy!"

The three men moved slowly toward the sofa like rusted metal toys, lowering themselves to its cushions as though they had to aim. They looked at me. I looked at them.

"Iggy," I said again.

Sugar laughed. Snipes glared at him as though he wished he would wither up into a ball of ash and blow away. Mr. Speegle sighed.

"I can tell you've heard the name before," Snipes said. "You probably already know that he's the man — the person — who your mother claimed, who she told me, us, was the father of her

— of you. Your father. Iggy Winslow. There's been some doubt about this, over the years, speculation that it wasn't Iggy at all, that your mother merely fabricated that story. And there've been rumors. Other men, at various times, have claimed to — well. A number of men say it's possible that they could have been the responsible party. Not that they're willing to *take* responsibility for it. But there's never been any way to prove it, really, one way or the other."

"Until now," Mr. Speegle said. "We were hoping we might be able to tell by looking. But you look like *her*. You're like an echo of her face, her eyes. Even her voice — I can hear her voice in your own."

"*Al,*" Snipes said. "After so long, you can understand, we were all eager to know who it was. But we don't have to know today. Unless, of course, *you* know, and want to tell us."

"Me?" I said. "Know what?"

"Who your father is," he said. "Perhaps he's been in touch. Written you letters. A phone call now and again?"

"No," I said. "Nothing like that."

"But you knew of Iggy," he said.

"Yes, but —"

"So what, then?" Sugar said. "You never had a daddy?"

"No," I said. "I had a father."

"Who was it, then?" Snipes said, leaning forward, hands on his knees. Sugar and Mr. Speegle sat up as well, their old, almond-shaped eyes as wide as they could get them, watching my lips now, waiting for an answer.

"My grandfather," I said.

And they nodded, exchanging looks, as if this made perfect sense.

This meeting went on for some time. Lucy brought us tea and tuna fish sandwiches. She glanced at me, briefly, turning away before anyone else saw me catch her eye. Mrs. Parsons stayed quiet. The three men speculated about one thing or the other without including me in their conversations. Much of the time I hadn't the slightest idea what they were talking about. At one point, for instance, Sugar said, "Aren't you going to ask him?" And Snipes said, "There's no reason to ask. The woman will tell us and then we'll know." "But aren't you even interested?" "Of course," he said. "But I'm not sure it's necessary to know that now."

The afternoon passed like this. The sun, setting somewhere outside the darkened room, shot a stray beam of orange light through a chink in the blinds, surprising me. Snipes, Speegle, and Sugar watched it as well.

"That's pretty," Sugar said, reaching out to touch it.

"It's the color of your mother's hair," Mr. Speegle said.

"Here we go again," Sugar said.

"For God's sake, Al," Snipes said. "Can't we just talk about what we've come here to discuss?"

"Of course," he said. "I just thought the boy would like to know that his mother, who died the day he was born, had hair the color of the setting sun."

"Well, now he knows," Snipes said. "And I'm sure he's thankful that you've provided this detail."

"Be still my heart," Sugar said.

Snipes looked at me and shook his head.

"This has always been the case," he said, apologetically, "where your mother was concerned: things in general just become more charged. Even after all these years."

"It's good to know, what Mr. Speegle said," I said. "That's why I'm here. I want to know."

"Her eyes were green," Mr. Speegle said. "Like yours."

"She had two of 'em, one on either side of her nose," Sugar said. "That's a whole handful of puzzle pieces right there. I got more too. She had arms, legs —"

"Thank you, Sugar," Snipes said.

"I'm not done," he said.

"Yes, you are," Snipes said. "There are other things — more important things — that we must discuss with Mr. Rider before we go any further."

"Things?" Sugar said.

"Plans," he said. "Regarding the festival."

Sugar coughed and adjusted his weight on the sofa cushions.

"Plans?" I said. "How could there be any plans regarding me? I just got here."

"The plans were made a long time ago," Snipes said. "For the day you did return."

"But no one knew I was coming," I said.

"We could hope," Mr. Speegle said, gazing at me fondly from above his glasses. "Never underestimate the power of hope, Mr. Rider. Who's to say but it was just that — our collective desire to see you — that drew you back to us?"

"No," I said. "It wasn't that. I came here because my grandfather died, and Anna —"

"Anna?" Snipes broke in. "Anna who?"

"Anna Watkins," Mr. Speegle said, his eyes widening as he understood. It was all as clear to him as a glass of water. A story seemed to unfold within his head, and he nodded as it did, as it made perfect sense to him. "She took you, and stayed with you all these years, didn't she?"

I nodded, drawn along by the tide of his thought.

"You must excuse me," he said, "but I've had a great deal of time to think about this. We all have. I've gone through a number of permutations. This one proceeds as follows: Anna Watkins raised you. After Lucy died she took Lucy's place. All these years perhaps you even thought that Anna *was* your mother. That's why you're here, isn't it? Anna sent you."

"No one sent me," I said. "I came because I wanted to."

"But she knew you would have to," he said, "once you found out."

"Which is why I never objected to that friendship," Snipes said, looking at Mr. Speegle. "I always knew something good would come of it."

"Nineteen years later?" Sugar said.

"Patience will bring with it a prize," Snipes said. "So it is written."

"By you," Sugar said.

"Someone had to," Snipes said. "But they were not my words. They just came to me. I told you that. I simply wrote them down."

He brought his hands together before him and rubbed them as though he were trying to start a fire. He seemed to be listening to his own thoughts now. I could almost hear his mind, the little parts inside of it turning, moving, making the big decisions. Then he smiled, but it was not a smile for me or for anybody else to see. He was in the process of being pleased with himself. "I'm sure this is all confusing to you, Thomas," he said. "I understand completely; how could it not be? But it's all going to become clear soon enough. Trust me. Please. The one thing you need to know — the important thing — is that it's all good. It's good you came back. It's good for you, for Ashland, for us all. With you here, I think we can resume, in a way, pick up where we left off all those years ago when your mother came." He looked at me, and then at the others, with a clear and growing sense of a bright expectation. "We need to tell everybody, today," he said. "The boy is back. We will have our festival. Again."

B ecause I was stubborn and curious, I decided to stay the night in the room dusted for me by Lucy. On the dresser, beside a vase of cut flowers, was a note. *I hope you enjoy your stay in our lovely town. Lucy.*

The next morning Mrs. Parsons told me I would be needed downtown for the festivities that kicked off the festival season, namely, the raising of the banner. The banner itself was to be tied, lamppost to lamppost, across the width of Main Street, and inasmuch as without me there would be no festival at all she encouraged me to attend every possible function associated with it, especially the seed-spitting contest, which she said had always been such a thrill for her and her late husband.

I hadn't slept well that night, though. Mrs. Parsons's house was air-conditioned, but by the time the air got to my room it was no longer cool, and the vents there just blew a dry and tepid air. All night I felt as though I were melting. Through sheer exhaustion I'd doze off for a minute or more, only to wake, sweating, wet sheets clinging to my thighs. Moonlight splashed across the still room. The stars burned with an archaic ferocity. I could see everything by the light of the moon: my jeans draped across the back of the wooden chair, the jagged cracks running through the paint on the ceiling, even the miniature pink flowers on the wallpaper. Sometimes I could hear things: the distant sound of sustained activity, of hammers and nails, of men and women engaged in a sweaty effort somewhere beyond the trees, as though life in this town never stopped to rest, or maybe it was a different sort of life that began after dark. I looked out my window to investigate. I could see a glowing light in the distance. Once, toward morning, I thought I saw someone in the yard below my window, a lone figure just standing there, staring; I think it was a woman. But as soon as I saw her she seemed to disappear, blend into the shadows, gone. A minute passed. Then another. Time moves slower at night, when you should be asleep. The heat seemed hotter. It almost drove me crazy.

I arrived in town early. A few people had begun to gather on a corner; others milled about right in the middle of the street, slowly moving out of the way when a car drove by. Ladders had been placed against the lampposts on either side of the street, but the banner itself remained folded in a large, tight triangle. Shopkeepers stood by their doors, children peered out of windows, and townsfolk greeted each other excitedly, laughing and slapping one another on the back.

Ashland wasn't much of a town, really. It was the kind of town you see in movies, the kind with no more than two city blocks of low brick buildings flat-lining against the sky. Parking was on the diagonal, and the streets were divided by islands of grass and trees. Anna had described it for me, and it turned out she remembered it well. What was more remarkable was how little it had changed in all that time. Ashland was like a machine made up of the same old used parts. Doors squeaked on their hinges, old cars backfired, and the bricks that made the buildings themselves appeared to have been recycled from buildings older still, the way their edges were chipped, cracked and worn, and the way the red had deepened over time to look like iron. Here within these two blocks there was a store for every common human need: food, clothes, hardware, drugs, books, and gifts. There was the church in the distance, and there was the courthouse, possibly remodeled or rebuilt more recently than any other building in town; Anna hadn't mentioned it. Its garish concrete modernity stood in stark contrast to the simple red-brick buildings surrounding it. The courthouse was so ostentatiously grand that it actually bestowed a kind of grace on the rest of the town, as though it were a reminder of what the rest of the world had become.

I drifted down the sizzling streets in a dreamy, sleep-deprived haze. Already, watermelon-shaped flags were hung from street lamps and posters announcing the festival appeared in shop windows. There was a kind of electricity in the air, an expectancy. Even I felt it.

Ahead of me, a crowd was forming. I walked to its edge, unnoticed. Straining to peer over the top, all I could see was the edge of a Plexiglas case, and nothing more. There was a boy beside me, about ten. His hair was the color of vanilla ice cream. He said, either to me or to himself, because he wasn't looking at me, "I bet it'll break a thousand."

"A thousand what?" I said.

"A thousand *what?*" he said, turning toward me, and laughed once, amazed. "A thousand seeds! It's a big one. I've seen it. Not so wide as it is long. That says something." He nodded sagely.

"A watermelon?" I said. "That's what we're looking at? Longer means more seeds, I guess. Right?"

He turned and looked me over, up and down, glowering. "You're not from around here, are you?" he said.

"Actually," I said, "I think I am. I just haven't been back in a while."

"Well, here's a news flash for you: we're having a festival. First time since my mama was a girl. We got a king and everything, just like in the old days."

"Is that right?" I said.

"Yep," he said. "He just come to town. He just —" The boy took a long, low look at me then, his eyes widening. "It's you, ain't it?" he said. "You're him."

"I don't know about that," I said, backing away a little bit.

He stood there, staring, frozen in the moment. He wasn't listening to me anymore.

"Can I . . . touch you?" he said. "Just like, you know, on your arm?"

"Sure," I said, thinking, *What's the harm?* "If you want to."

And he reached out and touched me with the tips of his fingers, not breathing at all. Then he turned and ran from there as fast as he could. In the distance I heard him scream with a frightened kind of joy: "I touched him!"

I made my way gradually to the front of the crowd. And there, like the Hope Diamond, a beautiful green and yellow watermelon was on careful display in front of Robert's Five and Dime, locked in a see-through box. It *was* quite long. A photo display of watermelons from the past and the ultimate seed count from each was posted on the stand beneath the watermelon, but only once had the seed count broken a thousand. That was in 1963, and it had contained 1,122 seeds. Most of the others were in the 800–975 range. The last picture was from the year before I was born. Seed count: 923.

Suddenly there was a man beside me. He gripped my arm and pulled my head down so he could whisper in my ear.

"Sometimes," he said, "the number will come to you, as if in a dream. People say that. Some people say that if you listen hard enough, you can hear the number, in the wind." He paused, letting it sink in, still slightly nodding. "Some people just guess." He smiled. "Follow me," he whispered. "Inside. I have something important to tell you."

He was a small, bald man, and he walked with miniature steps ahead of me into the Five and Dime. Against my better instincts, I followed. It was dark but for one glowing fluorescent light in a corner. In front of me was aisle after aisle of toys and gadgets, of games and glue, dim in the darkness. The man looked at me, nodding, as if the sight of me alone told him something he'd been hoping to know.

He smiled. His face was small and flat and blank. His eyes bounced around like little balls as he looked me over. I felt his eyes over the length of my entire body. He spent most of the time on my face, though. The skin around his eyes crinkled while he stared.

"A watermelon is ninety-two percent water," he said as he examined me. "That's what determines its size, the amount of water it gets while it's growing, not the number of seeds inside it. But you don't want to go telling people things like that. They don't want to hear it. There are a lot of things like that around here." He winked.

"Okay," I said.

I thought I should play it safe now and agree with whatever he said, because I was frightened, suddenly unsure of why I had allowed myself to be dragged inside this empty store by a stranger. I felt a very urgent need to get out. I felt safer in a group of crazy people than I did alone with just one.

"Listen," I said. "I should be getting back. They're expecting me. I don't know who you are or what you want with me, but they're raising the banner and —"

"For instance," he said, still nodding. "My store here. This is my store. It's called Robert's Five and Dime, right? It's been here for sixty years, a good fifteen years before I was even born. The man who started it was named Eddie Roberts; my name is Robert Owens. Completely different people. Not even related. But it's *still* Robert's Five and Dime. Get it?" He shook his head. "Some of the young people think this store has always been mine, and you can't tell them any different. It's like trying to convince a kid that the watermelon is a vegetable."

"It's not a vegetable," I said. "It's a fruit."

"See?" he said. "I don't even try anymore." He laughed and cocked his head to one side and looked at me, hard. "I think I know who your father is," he said.

"My father?" I said.

"I think I know," he said.

"So," I said. "Tell me. Who? Is he — is he still alive?"

"He is," he said. "Very much. At least he appears to be. By which I mean, I think it's me, Thomas," the little bald man said, whispering suddenly. "I really do. *I think it's me.* I'd always wondered — you know, all it takes is one time, right? And me and Lucy, there *was* that one time. We had a go at it. Sure we did. I never really knew; no one did. But then I saw you this morning and I thought, *Maybe. I might just be his dad.*"

"Might be?" I said. "You're just guessing?"

"It's the limp," he said.

"The limp," I said. "You have a limp too?"

"No," he said. "I *don't* have a limp. But my father did. And *his* father didn't. But *his* father — my great-grandfather — *did.* Get it? It's a limp that skips generations. It skipped me and hit you. That's what I'm thinking." He looked hard at me, still nodding.

"But there doesn't seem to be —"

"The slightest resemblance between us," he said. "No. But that's not how it works. Science is tricky. It doesn't always make sense. Otherwise we'd still be monkeys, wouldn't we? We'd still be sleeping in the trees."

"I guess," I said.

"So what's the problem?" he said. "Can't you give your old daddy a hug?"

He opened his arms and wrapped them around me. The top of his head stopped at my chest. I felt obliged to hug him back.

"It's a big day," he said, pulling away, looking me over. "It's a big day for me, for you, for this whole town. I'm *proud* of you, son, proud of you having the guts to come back here and jump-start the festival, and get us out of this mess we've been in for so long. It feels good, being your dad. If I am your dad. And I think I am, based on the limp. And your guts. We both have guts. You had the guts to come back and I have the guts to walk outside right now and tell this whole town what I think, that I'm your dad and you're my boy. I do. But I'm not going to do that, as much as I want to and as easily as I could. I have a family, Thomas. I have a wife, a daughter. What happened between your mother and me was a long time ago. There's no way I can claim you as my own without destroying everything I have. I hope you understand. It's going to have to be between the two of us. We're going to have to take this to our graves, Thomas. You hear me?"

"I hear you," I said. "Sure, I hear you."

"That's my boy," he said, and slapped me hard, once, on the shoulder. "Now get out there and raise that banner. Make me proud."

He wasn't my father. I mean, there was absolutely no way. I knew when I met my father — my true father — I would *know* it, that there would be something inside of me — something like an otherwise unused organ, a cellular cacophony — that would alert me to his presence, and I didn't feel it inside the Five and Dime. Robert Owens was just a man who said he had had sex with Lucy Rider, which, in and of itself, fell under the heading of Too Much Information. I walked back outside, confused, into the bright sunlight and sudden heat as though into a wall. It was a little before ten in the morning, and already the sun was beating down on the streets with a relentless intensity. By the time I got to the corner, which was only half a block away, sweat soaked my shirt and socks.

By now, a crowd of about fifty people had gathered. A dozen, many of them drinking coffee, were loosely gathered around the base of a ladder, on top of which stood a man who was tying the banner ropes to a lamppost, while the rest were scattered along the sidewalk in little groups.

"Ladies and gentlemen, may I have your attention!"

It was Carlton Snipes. He was standing on a wooden milk crate in the middle of the street. He was wearing a short-sleeved white shirt, and no tie, gray trousers. His armpits soaked the sides of his white shirt dark. He was a pointy man and he looked even pointier, standing on that crate, looking down at us.

"This is a wonderful day for Ashland," he said. "A day we've been waiting for and hoping for for a good, long time. Friends, I am happy to be standing here on this wooden box to tell you that *those days are over!* What was written has come to pass. Ashland is back! And why? All because of one young man. A young man who — whether he knows it or not — has it in his power to restore Ashland to its glory, to make the past present again. Ladies and gentlemen, allow me to present to you the link between what we were and what we are going to be. Let's open our homes and our hearts to a son of Ashland, and Lucy Rider's son, Thomas Rider!"

The townspeople erupted in applause, shouting and whistling. He had spotted me at the edge of the crowd and waved me over to his wooden box. As I came forward he stepped down and I stepped up, and I stood where he had before, above them all. I waved at them — I didn't know what else to do — and they clapped for me, and above us the banner suddenly unfurled, and the crowd clapped louder as the message was revealed, until a circuslike atmosphere prevailed, couples jumping and dancing around, hurling each other in crazy circles and pointing at the sign above them.

ASHLAND'S ANNUAL

Watermelon Festival!

JULY 21, 2001

***

Oldest in the Nation!
Come and See the King!

After a few minutes of standing there I stepped down from the box and moved away from the gathering. No one seemed to notice me anymore. They were too involved in their own carrying-on, their wildness, their nearly insane-sounding yapping and yelling.

My God, I kept thinking to myself, *my God my God my God,* as each new wild and freakish occurrence paraded in front of me. I had always felt that the world presented itself to me in a plain brown wrapper and that opening it and seeing what was there, touching it, smelling it, was all it took to understand it. But this is not the way it worked in Ashland. I was lost. Take a man and drop him in the middle of a three-ring circus and tell him that this was the way real people lived: it's how I felt then. I thought of Anna, back at the farm, all alone. I shouldn't have left her. *I should go back to her now,* I thought, and I brightened considerably at the prospect. But as I turned to leave the crazed group of hoppers and screamers, a man's hand settled on my shoulder and held me back, his breath warm on my neck.

"Thomas," he said into my ear, in a backwoods country lisp and stutter. "Thomas Rider. Maybe you don't know me, but I know you. I am the closest thing you got to a friend here, and I think you're the closest thing I got. So listen. There is some things I got to tell you. What I know about. Like where you come from, and where you're going. I want to get that part out right quick, before somebody comes. 'Cause you need to know. It's about the king, Thomas. The Watermelon King. You heard about him, didn't you? We have to have a king for the festival and he's called the Watermelon King, and I'm full of fear as to who that's going to be."

Though I'd never heard it before, I knew that voice. I knew the shape his hand would take on my shoulder. And turning to look, as I did then, I knew his hideous face.

"*Iggy,*" I said.

"Of course Iggy," he said. And he scanned the crowd nervously, his eyes slamming back and forth behind his slits. "I got to tell you about the king. Maybe you know. He's on the last float," he said, stuttering slightly, almost whispering. It's as if we'd known each other, somehow, the way he just started talking, chewing on something — tobacco? Grass? I couldn't tell. "There's lots of floats, though. I can name them. There's the Kiwanis, the Chamber of Commerce, the Affiliation of Downtown Businesses, Daughters of the Confederate Dead, Daughters of the Union, Children of the Free State of Ashland — and — then — this one. The one with the king." His mouth opened a little in his version of a smile. "He's sitting in a big chair," he said. "His scepter — it's called a scepter, you know — is a dried watermelon vine, and his crown is a hollowed-out watermelon rind. He has to wear the rind on his head, so he looks like, you know, an idiot. No matter what he looks like in real life. With a rind on your head, even you, Mr. Thomas Rider, even you would look like an idiot. It's a celebration and a shaming, all at once. Celebrated because of what you're about to do for the town, and shamed 'cause you're in the position to do it."

He tried to smile again. I looked at the ground. He was wearing mud-splattered blue tennis shoes, one of which wasn't tied. The ends of its laces, dragging the ground, were covered in mud.

"*No one* wants to be the Watermelon King, of course," he said. "No one wants to sit on that float with a rind on his head. I didn't. I would have done anything not to be the Watermelon King. But the thing is, you don't have to do *anything* not to be the king; you only have to do one thing. Or maybe I should say it like this. To be the king, it's not what you've done, it's what you haven't done that makes it all possible." His voice purred urgently in my ear.

"Okay," I said.

"To be the king . . ." he said, laughing again but speaking even more softly, as though this were a secret, the biggest of them all. "Are you listening, Thomas? Are you? You have to be a *virgin*. You have to *not* been with a woman. This is a true fact. It's one of those things no one talks about but everybody knows. This is not, I mean, *not* the information you'll find on one of the fliers they hand out at the chamber of commerce or anywhere else. But it is true. It's one of our traditions. The Watermelon King is the last one of all the men in Ashland — the oldest of the young, or the youngest of the old. It's like, you know, you *shouldn't* be a virgin, but you *are*, and it's funny. It's funny, kind of, to everybody but the king."

"This doesn't happen," I said. "Maybe a long time ago, but not anymore."

"No?" he said. "Not really? Then why is your mama dead?"

I shook my head. He knew what I wanted to know. "Why?" I said.

"Because she didn't believe it either. She didn't think there was such a thing, and when she found out she did everything she could to stop it, and she stopped it good. Because who wants it to happen that way? Who wants to go out into the field with the whole town knowing it, and do what it is you do? Not for the first time. Right?" He looked down at the street. "My shoe's untied," he said, but he didn't move to tie it. He just looked off into the hazy white sky, a thought, like a fly, buzzing around in his head. I could almost hear it.

"It was me," he said, thinking back to the time. "Almost. I was almost the Watermelon King one year, so many years ago now it's like another life ago, or like that was part one and this part two. That's how long ago and far away. *It was just about to happen.* Just about. It would have been . . . terrible, though. I don't think my constitution could have stood it. I'm weak that way," he said, standing taller all of a sudden, "*fragile.* I'm sensitive, because somewhere in me, somewhere inside this body you can hardly stand to look at, I have a soul of immense proportions. I do. That's what your mother said. That's what your mother told me, and I've never forgotten it. She saw it. 'A soul of immense proportions.'"

"*My mother?*" I said, almost stuttering myself.

He was watching me now, his eyes glowing.

"Your mother," he said, whispering, "your mother was the sweetest woman ever in the whole world. I'm sure you know that, and if you don't I'm telling you that it's so. It's not a secret. I don't know what would have happened to me if I hadn't met your mother." He looked at me, and his tongue moved around in his mouth like he had something in his teeth. But he wasn't looking at me. He was looking for her, in me. "I mean in the big picture, in the long term. Short term, of course, I know what would have happened real well. I would have been the king. If it hadn't been for your mother, I would have been the god-god-god-dern Watermelon King of 1982."

Now I looked up at his face, and he winked at me, or rather one of his thin slits snapped shut then opened again. And I couldn't tell what was in his brain, what was happening behind those eyes, if anything. But I did not see a *soul of immense proportions.*

He shook his head. "She knew, the way nobody else knew, that I couldn't have had a life after being the Watermelon King. Not even the kind of life I was set up to have, which was always going to be kind of shitty. It's that fragile part I mentioned before. So she . . . we . . . Well, you know," he said and laughed, "it's embarrassing to talk about. It ain't right to talk about in the day like this. This is night talk. But let's just say we took care of business. *She* took care of it. And it was . . . it was beautiful. In every possible way. How she saved me."

"My mother," I said. "My mother and you?"

"That's right," he said.

"And so somebody else was king that year," I said, but I was still thinking about my mother. And Iggy. The image of this man and my mother together in my mind.

"No," he said. "You'd think they'd find somebody else. You'd think that. Not that I cared, of course. A normal man might be able to stand it. I don't know. But no. They couldn't find one that year. Not in time anyway. After that, well, it's like those commercials: before and after. There was a before and there was an after. *This* is the after. What you see here. I'm sure you heard all about it by now. After is when the crop went bad and stayed that way. No more watermelon festivals. People moved away. And that's my fault, I guess. People been treating me like it's my fault for the last nineteen years anyway. Like I meant to hurt somebody, when I was only trying to save myself. And I am all sorry about it too. But you know: it beats being the king. I don't regret it, nothing about what happened. Except, of course, the last part."

"The last part?"

"The part," he said, "where your mother dies," and I looked at him long enough to see his eyes water up until he blinked the tears away. "She saved me," he said. "But now, with you back, it's all starting to happen again. There's talk, Thomas. See, the thing is, you don't look so much like me. People are making up their minds about that. They're going to start thinking maybe, you know —" and he looked away and blushed — "maybe I'm not your dad. Which means they'll start thinking I wasn't really with her. Which means —"

"You'd be the king," I said.

"*Again,*" he said.

"I don't understand, though," I said. "Why are you telling this to me?"

"'Cause you got to help me, Thomas," he said. "Like *she* did. You got to keep it from happening."

"But what can *I* do?"

"I don't know," he whispered. "But you're smart. I'm an idiot. Well, maybe not an idiot. But I'm not smart. Not as you. Just figure something out, Thomas. Like mother, like son, okay? I'm your friend — that's all I'm saying. That's all you need to know. I got your back. Now be mine. My friend. *Please.*"

As he turned and began to shuffle off, Sugar appeared behind him and grabbed him around his neck with one of his big arms. Sugar laughed, and Iggy gasped for breath.

"Morning, Iggy," Sugar said, and he let go. "Morning, Mr. Rider."

"Sugar," Iggy said. "Hey, Sugar."

"You boys look like you're engaged in riveting conversation," he said. "What in the world could you be talking about?"

"Nothing, Sugar," Iggy said meekly, backing away.

"Nothing?" Sugar said. "Okay. Okay now. But you been talking about nothing for a while. And Thomas here, he looks like he just swallowed a bird."

"Nothing big, I mean," Iggy said. "The Watermelon Festival and whatnot. Cucumber beetles. The squash vine borer. Pickleworm."

"Pests," Sugar said. "There are lots of pests afflicting the watermelon, aren't there?"

"That's right," Iggy said, and he caught my eye and winked. "Pickleworm and other pests. The enemies of the watermelon."

"Bacterial wilt," Sugar said, shaking his head as if he'd seen enough bacterial wilt to last a lifetime. "Anthracnose. Downy mildew."

"Downy mildew," Iggy said. "Oh, yeah. I'd forgot about downy mildew."

"That's what did us in, I think," Sugar said as the sweat poured down his face. "The downy mildew. That and the other thing."

"The other thing," Iggy said, chewing hard on whatever he was chewing on. "That sure didn't help, did it?"

The two of them exchanged a look. Then Sugar pounded Iggy, once, on the arm.

"That hurt, Sugar," Iggy said.

"It was meant to," Sugar said.

Then a word, an idea, maybe a whole conversation took place as they stared at each other. Sugar looked at me.

"What?" I said.

"Nothing," Sugar said. "Nothing at all. Something just occurred to me."

"Oh. Me too," Iggy said.

"I wanted to ask you yesterday, but Snipes wouldn't let me."

"What?" I said.

"Well . . ." he said.

"Go ahead and ask," Iggy said. Iggy was different now. Sugar's presence had changed him somehow. "Won't be the last time somebody asks him during his summer visit to Ashland."

"It's rude," Sugar said.

"Being rude is not so bad," Iggy said.

"Maybe not," Sugar said. "Have you ever . . ." he said, trailing off, looking at his shoes.

"What?"

"You know," Sugar said.

"You *know*," Iggy said.

"You're eighteen years old, aren't you?"

"That's right," I said.

"Okay now."

"Okay," said Iggy, like an echo.

"That's more than old enough if you ask me," Sugar said.

"More than plus some," Iggy said.

"So," Sugar said. "Have you?"

"Sure he has, Sugar," Iggy said, and he placed one of his hands on my shoulder. "A good-looking boy like this. Sure. A bunch of times. No way he hasn't. No way!"

"Been around the block a couple of times at least," Sugar said, smiling real big now. He reached out and took my shoulders in his hands and straightened me out until I was facing him head-on, and he stared. He stared into my eyes like a judge. "You can tell just by looking. That's what they say. Just by looking into somebody's eyes. It's all in there," he said, not blinking. "It's like a magic eight ball. Set still long enough and the answer just rises up."

And he stared into my eyes. But I shrugged his hands off my shoulders and turned away.

"Magic eight ball," I said. "Right."

"There's an old woman here," he said. "Lives by herself out in the woods. She can see it. She can see everything."

"I don't know what you're talking about," I said.

"You will," he said.

"You know," Iggy said.

"Sure you do," said Sugar.

"And if you don't, you will."

And Sugar laughed, and Iggy laughed, and I laughed too. I didn't know what else to do.

"It's none of your business," I said, "who I am."

And they laughed again.

"None of our business," Iggy said.

"We're going to have us a nice festival this year," Sugar said, looking away from me, toward something I couldn't see.

"A *nice* festival," Iggy said, nodding. "I for one can't wait."

Over the course of three days I spoke to whoever would speak to me, and, as Anna said would happen, learned more than I ever wanted to about my mother and about this town. I knew what was happening, though no one said it outright: I was the king. They thought I was going to be the king. I could see what they wanted in their eyes when they looked at me and with the things they said. But I wasn't going to let it happen. This was something I could say no to. I could go at any time. As soon as I had done what I came here to do — what I came here to learn about — I would leave, and I would know when that time came in my heart, because I would feel it. I would be a man then.

As for my father, it appeared I had several. During my first four days there, I met half a dozen volunteers, men who took me aside and swore me to secrecy and then told me a breezy, nostalgic tale about the night of love they'd shared with Lucy Rider, unnecessarily enumerative and explicit in their descriptions and determinedly — shockingly — salacious. They would look at me hard in the dark room we had moved to for their private disclosure, hold me by the shoulders, proud that I had become such a tall and handsome boy, the limp notwithstanding — it ran in the family, after all. And if it wasn't the limp it was some other part, either their ears or their eyebrows or their chin or their hands or their smile. But most often it was the limp, my clearest flaw, that they claimed as proof that I was theirs. But no one else must ever know, they told me, it was just between us, and I shook the hand of father after father, promising to keep it a secret forever.

In Ashland, the dense, moist heat was constant. Gnats crowded the morning air, and mosquitoes attacked with a mindless ferocity all night long. I did a lot of walking, more than usual, and the gap in the length of my legs caused me to have a strange throbbing pain in my groin. Sometimes the pain woke me up at night, and when it did I would lie in bed and all I could think about was sex. Sex was what Ashland was all about — having it, not having it, and the consequences of both. So I thought about sex, of having sex, of other people having it with other people, and other people having it with my mother. Of Iggy. And then me, not having it with anybody, ever. In the dark of the night I would look down at my penis. The reality was it had failed me. It was a pitiful thing, small and soft and ridiculous. Not once in the presence of a woman had I felt it charge up, the way I knew it should. There should come a point in a man's life when his brain and his heart shuts down and his cock takes over; it's what being a man is about. Then, later, you learn how to work them all at once. But it was a mystery to me. To compound the mystery, I'd had my chances. I was not without a component of desire. Maybe my mother had left a message in my soul, a Post-it note on my personality, telling me not to go where she had gone. Or maybe not to go there just yet.

Back at Mrs. Parsons's one afternoon, there were some women sitting in the back of her parlor. I could see their silhouettes against the blinds along the back wall, fading and blending in the shadowed light. I squinted but could not make them out clearly. Mrs. Parsons took me aside and whispered.

"These here women need to talk with you, Thomas," she said.

"To me?" I said. "What about?"

"Oh, nothing," she said. "Not really. They just want to talk.

And you don't have to say a thing. Just listen. Look and listen. And if one of them is particularly nice, you know, make a little note in your head. And if one of them isn't, make a little note about that too."

"Why?" I said.

"It's just part of the festival," she said. "Think of it that way. You're helping us . . . pick a queen."

"I don't know," I said. "I probably shouldn't get involved."

"Involved?" she said, and laughed. "It's a little late for that."

"Mrs. Parsons —"

"Sit down right here," she said, leading me over to the big chair, and one by one they came forward into the light.

"Hi," the first one said. She was just a girl, younger even than me, I think, with long brown hair and a halter top, cut-off jeans, flip-flops. Chewing a piece of gum. "My name is Becky." She paused, as if that's all she had planned to say and was hoping something might just come to her now. "Man, it's hot, ain't it? H-O-T hot. Even in the darkest part of the night." She stuck out her hand for me to shake, and I shook it, but she pulled it away quickly, and flapped it in the air as though it had gotten burned. "You can't hardly *touch* in this heat without breaking out into an uncontrollable sweat, can you? Not that I mind sweating if it's the right kind of sweat if you know what I mean. But this is misery. M-I-S-E-R-Y. Period. And it will only get hotter," she said. "Pretty soon, it's all people will be able to talk about. 'Hot enough for you?' they'll say. Or, 'You could fry an egg on this sidewalk.' 'A real scorcher.' 'One for the record books.' And some joker will come around and say, 'It's so hot, I just saw two trees fighting over a dog.' You hear that joke about seven hundred times in August. Eventually, it makes you want to kill yourself in an especially awful way."

She stood in front of me and twirled around so I could view her from every angle.

"Not *too* bad to look at, am I?" she said. "Probably not the least likely in that department. My folks think I'm easy and they might as well get some mileage out of it. The truth is, of course, I *am* a little easy," she said. "Easier than some, anyway, harder maybe than others. I keep thinking I'm not, but when the rubber hits the road — and I don't mean that kind of rubber, either, you dirty-minded boy! — I just . . . give it up! I can't help it." She ran her index finger back and forth across the side of her neck, where little beads of sweat dripped swiftly to her shoulders in its path. "When a guy touches me, right . . . *here,*" she said, "and kisses me, with his mouth and a little . . . a little tongue? I go absolutely insane." She looked at me matter-of-factly. "And that's all she wrote. After that, things begin to move at a pretty fast pace. It's like I'm possessed." She took a step closer, the tips of her fingers running smoothly across her chest. "It's like, there is no right and wrong, should or should not. It's just two people wanting to get out of their shells, becoming one person. That's all it's about, I think. Two people becoming one. Joined, brought together like that. That's why it feels so good. And it does," she said, moving closer. "It really does."

She looked over my head to the hallway behind me, where Mrs. Parsons was apparently directing. Becky looked disappointed.

"Well, I guess that's it." And she turned and slumped back into the shadows.

The next woman was older and taller. As her face moved into the light she squinted, and I could see the crow's-feet in the corners of her eyes. Her hair was short and black, and badly cut, as though with dull scissors, and her skin was the color of chalk.

"My name is Julie," she said in a soft voice, and, smiling, turned away. "I'm different from most girls, I guess. Not that there's anything wrong with that. With being different. We got lots of different in Ashland, you know. My little sister crawls around on the floor like an animal. I think she has a learning disability, but it's hard to say. My little sister, she collects the ragged little black and red bodies of the mosquitoes she kills. She has jars full of them. Different, but that's okay to people 'round here. There's a man on my street who stuffs and mounts all his dead pets, and on a nice day he'll set 'em out in his yard, just so, so it's like they're playing together. Dogs and cats and a little parakeet he sets on a tree branch. That's fine with us. And then of course there's Iggy Winslow. You couldn't ask for someone more different than him. He mows a dead lady's lawn. My daddy sits in his big chair and reads the paper and watches television and my mother sits on the couch, cutting coupons and going through recipe books to find something really tasty to cook, although it all ends up tasting about the same. They never talk.

"So it's not being different that we have trouble with. It's the *kind* of different I am. I am a thirty-year-old woman and I have never been with a man because I have been waiting for you to come back. People — boys especially — have always thought that's a little odd. How I could lock my prize away just thinking about the day you'd come back. People knew the story, but they had no faith. I did. I waited. Now what are they thinking? I am the Least Likely because I am the *most* likely; I am the One True Believer. I am pure because I have saved myself for you, Thomas Rider, son of Lucy. Everything we have is gone. We live with this fact on a day-to-day basis. My earliest memory is watching the parade go by, all the floats made by everybody and truck after truck full of the biggest, juiciest watermelons you've ever seen. It's something that's passed down in our blood, I think. Like an instinct. And seeing the Watermelon King, with that rind on his head and holding the pitiful old vine, and waving at us all as he passes. I want that feeling again. And then I want you planting your seed inside of me. That's what I want most of all, more than anything. You inside of me. Please."

She bowed, slightly, and wandered back into the shadows. In the darkness, no one could see me blush.

After a moment, the third woman walked out. Young. She

185

presented herself in silhouette, her face edging into the light from the darkness, and she nodded in my direction.

"Mr. Rider," she said. "My name is Kara, but other than that I don't know what to tell you. Nothing about me is really important except for this, the real reason I'm here."

She turned to show me the other side of her face. Across her cheek, from the top of her ear to the bottom of her chin, was a long pink scar. It looked like a piece of rope had been buried beneath her skin. I couldn't help it: seeing it there, I flinched.

She smiled.

"There you go," she said. "It's no mystery, then, is it, why I'm here. It happened when I was six. I was walking along the top edge of the sofa, like a little acrobat. When I fell, I hit the coffee table and knocked it over, and there was a big glass of tea on it. It hit the floor and shattered, and then my face hit the glass. And it shattered." She glanced at me and shook her head.

"I do not suggest having a scar across your face to those women interested in a vital social life. Certainly, it's given me time to read. I am a big reader, Mr. Rider. But in matters of the heart, this" — she touched her scar — "has always gotten in the way. I have loved. I've never touched, but I have loved. My mom always said that if I act pretty, people will think I'm pretty, but she was wrong. Love does *not* conquer all; I can attest to that. Love cannot even conquer *this*. And if it can't conquer this, what good is it?

"Now all I want is to be part of a story myself. As the ugliest girl in Ashland, it seems only appropriate. That's all we *are* is stories, anyway. You know that by now. That's all we have left. War stories, Negro stories, watermelon stories, *love* stories. That's what I want. To be with you would be another chapter in the story."

She came closer to me now, closer than any of the women had before her, and she got down on her knees in front of me and stared, forlorn, into my eyes.

"Do you ever feel like a ghost, Mr. Rider? I mean, invisible? Or not exactly invisible, but not being seen for who you are? The rest of the world is busy going on about its business, and you're in the middle of it but at the same time outside of it all, watching everything and everybody, wanting to be known, to cry out, screaming, *Hey, I'm here! Here I am!* But like in a dream you can't scream, can't do anything but hope somebody notices you, sees you the way you want to be seen, to be known?"

I nodded.

"Touch me," she said.

"What?"

"Touch me," she said, and closing her eyes she held out her sun-browned arm. I reached out, slowly. I was about to rest my fingers on her arm when I looked up at her face, full on both sides for the first time. She looked like two different people. "Go on," she said, smiling, her eyes still closed. "Touch me. That's all it takes, sometimes. Being touched."

I touched the scar. She shuddered and lost the smile, and though I could tell she wanted to open her eyes she fought against it, kept them shut tight, and she breathed in short, staccato bursts.

"And voilà," she said, opening her eyes and looking at me dead-on, fearlessly. "I'm not a ghost anymore. For now. I want this same feeling, but forever."

"Mrs. Parsons," Lucy said, calling through the screen door and opening it, walking in.

"Not now, Lucy!" she said.

But either she didn't hear her or it didn't matter if she did, because she came right into the room anyway, and saw us, me and the woman on her knees before me, my fingers touching her face.

"Well, well," she said. "Is this how the white people do it?"

"*Lucy,*" Mrs. Parsons said.

"Hey, Lucy," I said, and tried to smile so that she could see it.

And the blood inside my body suddenly turned warm. Because there was something that she did to me, just looking at her, knowing she was close. That was all I did, of course: look, pass her in the hallway on the way to supper, smell the scent of her in my room after she'd cleaned it, her presence everywhere, in this house, on my mind, her note in my pocket. We hadn't yet exchanged a word.

On my sixth night in Ashland, on the eve of the festival it-self, there was what was called the Night of the Past Kings, a gathering of all the former Watermelon Kings in a banquet room on the second floor of the Steak and Egg. Mrs. Parsons said they were expecting me, so I went. I walked up the carpeted stairs. Sugar sat in a metal folding chair in the hallway outside the door. His body seemed to engulf it; the chair looked ready to disappear into his ass. When he saw me he smiled, and the cigar dangling from the corner of his mouth appeared to wave.

"Hi, Sugar," I said.

"They told me you was coming," he said, and winked. "Go on in. But don't think 'cause I'm sitting here that I was ever a damn king. I had a taste of the good life first time when I was fourteen and I haven't stopped since. I'm just the doorman, so's you know. The keeper of the keys."

"I see," I said.

He winked again and adjusted his weight against the bottom of the chair.

"Scared?" he said.

"Scared? No," I said, though I was, a little. I knew why I was wanted here.

"Good for you," he said, smiling. "Now go on in and have yourself a time."

Inside the room there were between forty and fifty men, all dressed in gray suits and brown suits and wearing old ties and shiny black shoes. I wore the nicest clothes I'd brought with me:

brown corduroys, a white shirt with a button-down collar, and my newest pair of blue sneakers. Mrs. Parsons thought I could do better, but there wasn't time to make any significant improvements. It was time to go and so, somewhat reluctantly, I went. There were half a dozen tables, all of them round and covered in beige cloth. At the center of each was a watermelon, whole, a small one so that it fit on the table, and stuck to the top of it was a plastic, golden crown.

The entire room turned to look at me when I came in, but only for a moment. Some of them waved, some of them smiled and called my name, and some leaned in close to the men at the table next to them and whispered, I don't know what, and then they would nod to one another, knowingly, and look back at me. I had seen all these men before, it seemed, walking the streets of Ashland, carrying on the business of their lives like normal people, seemingly no different than the other men who had managed to avoid their fate. Shopkeepers, merchants, workers. Fathers, husbands, sons. I couldn't tell now what had made them special, like me, what had caused them to fail in the surrender of their virginity. Scattered about were several of the men who had claimed to be my father over the course of the last few days. Some were sitting together, talking. They all smiled at me, but otherwise weren't, for the most part, very fatherly.

After my presence was taken in, the room returned to normal. Men chatted, hunched over and nodding, with the other men at their little round tables. Music, so distorted that it was hardly recognizable as such, blared from a tiny tape player in the back of the room. The ceiling lights were dim. I walked between the tables, looking for a seat, taking in the rest of the scene.

The oldest king was eighty-three. He was the king of kings and he sat in a rocking chair on a slightly elevated platform and rocked, all by himself, his dinner beside him on a fold-out tray.

He looked out across the room with a possessive benevolence, as though it were filled with his children, and the children of his children. He fell asleep a few minutes after I arrived.

Finally, I found an empty seat, and it happened to be at the table of the youngest Watermelon King of them all, the king from the last year the festival was held, twenty years ago, Joshua Knowles. He was thirty-nine years old. He was small, and small boned, gentle-looking with scarily white skin, and he kept his head lowered, close to his salad bowl, as though he were afraid some of his French dressing might drip onto his suit.

"Hi," I said.

"Oh. Hi," he said, barely looking up at me.

"I'm Thomas Rider," I said.

"I know who you are," he said. He looked into my eyes, and then, searchingly, at the pocket of my shirt. He scowled, and then looked back into my eyes.

"Where's your number?" he said.

"My number?" I said.

"On your nametag," he said. "Where's your number?"

He pointed at his. It said "3."

"I don't know," I said. "What's the number for?"

He motioned for me to move close to him so he could whisper.

"Women," he said. "It's for the number of women."

He nodded, edging his eyes away from me toward the men at the other tables around us. Each man had written a number on his nametag: 7, 12, 23, 42. It took me a minute, but I finally understood: it represented the number of women each man had slept with since their day as king. And this is what the party was really all about, I discovered: the men who were once celebrated for being virgins were here to celebrate the life they had lived since. As the night passed the men around me were congratulated, or ridiculed, for the number of their conquests.

"Twelve! I can't believe that. Last time it was three, you devil! You've been busy!"

"My wife is number twenty-three and I pray to God there's not a twenty-four."

"Four? I could do four in my sleep. In fact, I think I have!"

I drank a glass of white wine. Joshua had a few glasses more than that and got a little drunk.

"Hard to believe I was ever a king," he said sadly into his drink. "But they say that it's fate sometimes, that everything from birth on up is leading to that day, and in my case I think it was. I was fated to be the king. One thing leads to another and there you are."

"Was it really bad?" I said.

"Oh, it was terrible," he said, shaking his head. "Worst day of my entire life. I kept hoping *something* would happen, up to the very last minute. You know what I mean. I had a girlfriend, and we were talking about it, but it just . . . it just didn't happen. She was a Christian. I was too, but not that much. Not so much so that I wouldn't sleep with her. I mean, I got to third base a couple of times with Molly and was closing in on home, but in the end, I swear, it just didn't happen. That's why I think it was fate. I would have paid for it, you know, but that sort of thing is looked down on."

"It's bad for a whore to be your first time," an old-timer beside me chimed in. "Bad luck, I mean."

"Your John Thomas might fall off," someone else said. "Down the line somewhere, when you least expect it."

"There are men not here tonight who weren't kings because of some whore, who don't have their purple-headed trouser snake today."

"There are meatless men in Ashland," the first said. "That's just a fact."

"Not here, though," Joshua said, looking around him. "This is such a small town, there's only one whore and she knows you. She knows your parents. She won't do you, not for a hundred dollars. And you could drive down to Birmingham — some people have — but that seems wrong to me. For your first time, I think it should happen in the town where you live. If not, not. And then just move on. I moved on. Broke up with Molly. Had to. This last year has been a good one for me, though. I'm on number three," he said. "All real nice girls too. What about you?" he said.

I glared at him. "What about me?"

"Your number," he said.

"Oh," I said. "I'm not a past king."

"I know that," he said. "Still, I'd be interested. How many?"

"I don't know if that's something I want to talk about."

"Come on. How many women have you been with so far?"

I leaned over. "Actually," I whispered, "none."

"None?"

"Not one," I said.

"You kidding me?" he said.

I shook my head. "I'm not kidding," I said. "It's the truth."

"That's what I mean," he said, and he leaned in closer to whisper to me. "Why are you telling me the truth? Do you think anybody here is?"

"I don't know," I said.

"Hell no," he said. "I don't expect anybody is."

"Well, I don't lie very well," I said. "I never could."

"You should learn," he said, and winked at me. "It helps in the day to day."

The wine had warmed me to Joshua. "People figure me for the Watermelon King," I said, and he nodded. "But I'm not. I mean, I don't want to be. You're saying maybe I can lie and get out of it. Tell me more."

"Wish I could help," he said, shrugging his shoulders. "But in the final analysis, it doesn't matter. Not for what's happening tomorrow. She can look at you and tell. What you say doesn't matter."

"The swamp lady," I said.

Joshua shivered as his mind looked backwards.

"She's as old as dirt," he said in a dead monotone, "and that's how she looks. The skin on her face has dried up and stuck together, like a piece of crumpled-up paper covered in mud, and almost all her hair is gone, except for patches that jump out of her scalp. She hasn't been able to walk for about a hundred years, and so they have to go into the swamp and get her, two men, and carry her to town. She doesn't use her eyes because they're gone; where her eyes used to be are just black holes, full of ash. She doesn't need her eyes to find you, though. She tracks you, like a dog, the men carrying her through town, holding her and a light for them to see. She knows where you've been and where you're going. There's no escape at all. She finds you soon enough. She doesn't talk. She never says a word. I don't know that she speaks a human language. The men say what needs to be said. But once they've got you, once you realize there's nothing left to do but stand there and *be,* be who you are, her long bony arms rise from her matted wolves' clothing and in her hands she's holding the biggest watermelon you've ever seen, how she even has the strength to hold it in her hands is a mystery — but she does, she holds it in the air in front of you, shaking and shivering like she's about to explode until she drops it — bam! — right at your feet, and the red meat of the melon splatters like blood across your shoes and pants, and there is no going back then. You are who you are, and there is no going back. Such a thing has happened to every man here."

"Except me," I said, in a soft voice.

"Except you," he said, and smiled.

• • •

194

It was a quite a night. After dinner — a big steak and a baked potato, steamed carrots, rolls, and corn sticks, and banana pudding for dessert — awards were given out. There was a little prize for the man who had had sex the farthest away from Ashland — winner, Tokyo, Japan — and for the man who had had it with the most members of the same family, not his own. By midnight, everybody was drunk, and I was tired, so I slipped out. The hallway was empty; Sugar was gone. I was a little drunk myself, I discovered, as I stumbled over the sidewalk leading to the street. It was so dark I tripped over the curb. The lights on the lamppost holding the banner flickered and died as I walked under it, and the sky was full of dim stars, and no moon. Every window was dark. For a moment I could imagine Ashland as a ghost town, abandoned, given over to kudzu, the buildings surrounded by dense vines and huge leaves — a ruin.

I heard something, the crack of gravel, a ways away. When I turned, I didn't see anyone. But from beyond a corner, near the courthouse, I saw a light, a muted glow, hovering beyond the farthest wall. I stared for a moment, squinting, then turned and started back toward Mrs. Parsons's house. I glanced behind me but saw nothing. But then the same warm, yellow light cast a shadow in an alley up ahead. I think in fact I already knew, somewhere inside of me I knew, but my mind would not allow me to believe it. It was the old swamp woman.

Except you, Joshua had said. And I remembered him smiling.

I moved backwards from the light and began to run. When I turned around I could see dark figures some ways behind me, the light seemingly suspended in front of them, unsupported in the air, coming my way, but so slowly I almost laughed, because there was no way they could catch me like that. Still, I decided it was best to keep running. I ran back through town and into a neighborhood just beyond Main Street, cutting through yards and jumping fences, until I had to stop, and rest, and breathe, and when I did I discovered I had arrived at the place where I started from — and not tonight, but eighteen years ago. I was at the Hargraves place, and I saw, as though I had fallen into the heart of this town's ignorant superstition, a face at the broken window, staring into the darkened distance. But it was not Hargraves, and not my mother, either.

It was Iggy.

He saw me coming and moved away. Behind me was only darkness. I pushed the front door open, and I found him in the living room, sitting in a wooden chair, staring at a candle flame and the swarming bugs that surrounded it. He had a little stick in one hand, and he was dragging one end of it through the river of warm wax running along the floor. He didn't even look up when I came in.

"Kids come here sometimes," he said, "but I run 'em off. They got no business here. You would not believe the kind of things they do in this house. Upstairs. It's not right, after everything that happened. I tried to keep it all, you know, nice — the house and everything. Her daddy tore it up real good when he came down here after her. And then it got to be too much. Finally I just figured I'd stick with my expertise, you know, and keep the lawn mowed. Except for the patch of clover by the mailbox. Like I told you, your mama liked that patch of clover."

He looked at me, and his mouth made its little smile.

"She taught me to read right over there," he said, and pointed, with the stick, to the dining room, empty now except for a few dry leaves blown into a pile in the corner. "Coming here for those lessons, I was so happy. It was like now I knew the reason for *not* learning in the first place, for living all of my life and being treated the way I was, like a piece of dried-up crap, you know, by everybody, and not even being allowed in the regular classes. It was so I could have this happy part of my life. Those days sitting in that chair beside her, I was the happiest idiot you ever saw. I had more joy in me then than the smartest man in Ashland." He thought for a second. "Joy," he said. "I never thought I would have anything that would make me feel that way. But I did."

"You did?" I said. "You felt that joy?" And when he heard the accusation in my voice he jerked his head up and his body tensed as though he were going to come at me, but then he softened, turned away, and he looked into the candle again.

"Now," he said. "Don't you start. I got enough hate toward me. Anyway, I never got farther than her elbow," he said and laughed. "The rest was a damn story. Hers, not mine. I can't believe it worked. Not for a second. Even today, I can't. And I don't think anybody else really believed it either — I mean, me and your mama? Come on. But they didn't know for sure one hundred percent. There was *reasonable doubt,* like they say. They had to wait and see."

"So," I said, watching his face appear and disappear as the candle's light flickered. "You're not my father."

He laughed, and then took the laugh back, sucked it in like air.

"Do I look like your father?" he said.

In the candlelight, he turned his face to me and glared. No, he didn't look like my father. There was his terrible face and what I had thought were the shadows from the candles. He was covered in bruises, and one cheek was cut, the gash mottled with dried blood.

"Sugar didn't think I looked much like your father, either," he said, and, laughing, winced. "He figured there'd be more to you than a limp, given everything. He worked me over good for that. Worse than the first time."

"I'm sorry," I said.

"Not your fault," he said. "You can't help it that I'm not your daddy."

I looked at him.

"Then who is?" I said, not knowing if he knew anything at all.

"You know already," he said.

"I don't," I said.

"You do."

"Nope."

His voice was sharp and certain. He wouldn't look me in the eyes now.

"I'm not going to guess," I said. "It could be any man I've met since I came here."

"You don't have to guess," he said softly. "Because you know too. You know him."

"Then tell me," I said.

"I can't," he said.

"You can."

"I don't —" He looked at his shoes. "I don't want to come out and say it. It's hard."

"It's okay, Iggy," I said. "You can tell me."

"Don't want to."

"Is it Al?"

"No."

"Jonah Carpenter?"

"Not Jonah," he said.

"I'm not going to guess!" I said.

"You don't have to."

"Then tell me."

And I grabbed his frail shoulders — too hard — and turned him toward me.

"You're going to hit me, aren't you?" he said. "You're going to hit me, just like Sugar."

"I'm not going to hit you, Iggy," I said.

He nodded, slowly.

"I been hit enough," he said, "haven't I?"

"More than enough," I said. "Too much." I let him go. I watched the fear leave his face, and the beginning of a smile appeared.

"Feels good," he said, "not being hit." He rubbed his shoulders with his hands. "*Not* getting something, it's like *getting* something sometimes. Like a present. Thanks."

"Iggy," I said.

"I'm sorry, Thomas," he said. He reached out with his hand and touched my hair, pushed it back from my forehead.

"You're like me," he said. "But you're just learning how much you lost, and I already knew all this long time."

"What are you talking about, Iggy?"

"You was in her . . . before she got here, Thomas. She wore those nice open summer dresses so no one noticed. But I saw her up close all the time. So I knew, and toward the end she told me, because she couldn't hold it in anymore. Like you. One way or another, come time, it was all coming out."

He shook his head and opened his eyes so I could see them, full, for the first time. They were blue.

"Your father," he said, "is your father."

"*What?*" I said. "That doesn't —"

"It does," he said, moving away from me, breathing hard. "When you think about it, it does. Why she had to leave. Why she had to get away from home so bad. Why he never came to find her."

"But who — ?"

But then I stopped, because I knew. This wasn't a riddle, it was the truth, a thing hard to recognize because it had been so long since I had seen it.

"No," I said, shaking my head. "You can't know that."

"Thomas," he said, and he placed his hand on my shaking shoulder.

"I don't believe you," I said, knocking his arm away from me.

"I *should* hit you now for saying that, Iggy. I should beat the hell out of you."

"But you won't," he said. "You won't. Because that's not in you, Thomas. You got that sweetness in you. That sweetness, it runs in your family. But then when it turns on you, the sweetest things, you can get lost. That's how you need to think about all this. It's how she learned to think about it. Grief," he said, and he moved away from the wall and back to the candle. He picked up a toothpick and set it on the flame, and it burned. He pressed it to his arm where it burned for a second and then died. He didn't even flinch. "It happened in grief. And grief mixes people up. Lucy told me how it was. Her father was a good man, she said, *a good man*. And she was a good woman. But when the thing you love most is taken away, bad things happen, and you don't know why. His wife, her mom. Gone forever. Neither of them knew what they were doing. She couldn't explain it herself. For a time it's like comfort. Two people, holding on to each other because everything else is falling apart around you. I know how it happens. I've lost people. And she said, you just do it, once, and it's done, and then it becomes a time that lasts forever. For the rest of your life. Everything is dark, inside and out. That's the way it is with me most of the time. I just try to not trip over things. But it was harder for her. You know?"

"I know," I said, because it was dark all around me now. I felt like I was being swallowed up into the deepest hole, and that I would stay there forever. There were no words for how I felt just then, because feelings were all I had. Everything on the inside came out and took over, and it was black. Everywhere I looked was black.

"Didn't even tell Anna," he said, smiling and nodding to himself. "I reckon that makes me her best friend. I know a lot nobody else knew, for sure. They just thought she was a cold fish. Someone even wrote a little song about her. Wrote it on bathroom walls around town. It was like . . . it went like this. Let's see:

Lucy Rider, Lucy Rider
Does she have a heart inside her?
Or is it just a little heater?
Ice is warmer, salt is sweeter.

Not like they knew anything. Not like anybody in this town knows anything. The way they treated her, her and me both. Are you listening to me, Thomas? You look like you aren't listening to me. You got a lot to think about, I reckon. But I don't know what I ever did to end up this way. I was just being me. All of my life, I've just been me. But inside of me, I have all this *hate* now. For everyone, everyone in this town. Not you. Hey. Thomas? You got that look like you're not listening. I'm telling you something. Lucy Rider got me out of a tight spot, Thomas. A *real* tight spot. Just like you did. And for that, I have to say thanks. Thank you very much."

"You're welcome," I said, without knowing why. Coming back to the moment slowly, I looked down at him.

And then he blew out his candle, but there was no diminution of the light. Now it came from a different source.

Two men hidden beneath burlap hoods stood behind me. One held a candle. The other held what looked like a little black doll. That's what it was, actually: a doll, ancient, its stuffed arms and legs attached and reattached by thread, its face worn away by time, years in an attic somewhere, half-destroyed by moths.

But as I looked at it, I thought of my father, who I'd lost and gotten back again, who'd lived and died and lived and died again, and I saw what he would have seen. He would have seen the better story. What a liar my father was. Not only did he lie, he lied about lying. He told the truth and said *it* was a lie. Nothing was true or maybe everything was: a self-made man if there ever was one, Edmund Rider, the name itself a self-made thing. I wanted to make something of myself too, to outfox the past, so I didn't see an old doll. I saw the swamp woman, in the flesh. She was small as a child, and horrifically destroyed by time. More than old, she looked dead, her meager self charred, blackened by time. She looked as though she had been dead for a very long time, in fact, and had been dug up only for this occasion. Maybe she *was* dead and yet still lived somehow. She didn't move. She had no eyes, and her mouth was a wicked thin line across the bottom of her grizzled face, and it didn't move, either. Her arms moved a little bit, but maybe it was the men who held her who moved them.

"Thomas Rider," one of the men said. It was Sugar. There was no mistaking his voice; I could also see his nametag from earlier in the evening visible beneath the edge of the burlap itself. In his outside hand he held the lantern. "It is known that you have aged eighteen years plus some. It is also known that you have yet to be with a woman, to sow your seed in the furrow of her fields, yet to open the box where the seed is stored, that which is the beginning of us all, forever and forever. Is this true?"

He said it as though he'd said it before, many times, was in fact tired of saying it. I couldn't speak, still stunned by what I'd learned, by the withered figure in front of me and the two hooded men.

"Is this *true?*" the other man said, more insistently. Snipes. "You *must* answer the question."

"It's . . . true," I said. "I guess. I mean — I'm eighteen. Sure. But I've been with women. More than I can count. One from every state in this country. I have a wife in Texas. I —"

"You are the king," Snipes said, and suddenly, as though a switch had been turned, the old woman came alive, and from somewhere deep within the ancient folds of her ragged fur her bony hands brought forth a watermelon, one as big as any I'd ever seen, and she lifted it above her own head and in that moment her black eyeless sockets seemed to gleam a fierce and evil red, and she hurled it at my feet, where like a bomb it exploded, showering me in the red bloody meat.

"Then you are the king," Sugar said.

"The Watermelon King," Snipes said, and they turned and left, and when I looked back to Iggy I found that he was gone too, that I was alone, in the dark, in an old haunted house.

I woke the next morning and saw Mrs. Parsons standing above my bed, staring down at me, her eyes small and cold, a pair of scissors in her hand. Briefly, I considered whether last night had happened at all. Perhaps it had all been a dream.

"Get up, Thomas," she said. "It's time."

Though I'd tried to wash up after coming in last night, I found I was still covered in little brown seeds. I'd pick off one and find two more, as if they were multiplying on my skin, in my hair. And I felt sticky all over, as though I had taken a bath in the juice. Walking back through the dead and silent town the night before, I had thought I might leave Ashland in the morning; after all, most of my mysteries had been solved. There was just one more, and I thought I could figure that one out somewhere else.

I watched her walk stiffly to the door of my room.

"I need to call Anna," I said.

"Phones are down," she said.

"She's worried about me," I said. "I need to talk to her."

"Sweet boy," Mrs. Parsons said. "Don't you think she knew exactly what you'd be getting into if you came back to us? Doesn't she know what's going on? Really? What's your heart tell you about that?"

"I don't know that I can hear my heart," I said.

"Listen hard," she said.

"I could go right now," I said. "You can't keep me here."

She stopped, and turned.

"Your car is gone," she said.

"You're all loony," I said. "Every one of you. I could still leave," I said. "Run. Run until I get somewhere . . . normal."

"Start running, and you'll never stop," she said. "You should know that's true firsthand." She wore a cool, hard face, as though all the sweetness she had shown before had been a ruse. "And don't bother getting dressed. I'll fix you up with some clothes downstairs." She stared at me for a moment and smiled. "What's the worst that can happen?" she said. "You get to be with one of the women you met the other day."

Then she left me.

I put on an old man's green and red plaid robe I found lying on my bed and walked downstairs. She was standing behind a chair in the middle of the dining room, waiting.

"Have a seat," she said.

I didn't move. She held up the scissors.

"Haircut," she said. "Sit."

"But —"

"Thomas, you're the king now," she said. "You know it, I know it, everybody knows it. There's no sense objecting. All that's left is for me to make you look nice, and then you go into town so the rest of the women can get an eyeful. See what they're missing. They all want to see the merchandise close up, you know. Then the sun goes down, and you — well, you know the rest."

I did know the rest. But it wasn't going to be me. There was no sense in objecting to Mrs. Parsons. She was just doing what she thought was right. But there was still time, I thought, to change the end of this story myself. I was not going to be a victim of a fate I hadn't chosen, to the idea that each day from the day I was born was leading to this day, that each day from the day my father left Ashland had come to this. I would see it through, but I would do it by my own lights, not by theirs.

She cut. My hair fell in chunks to my shoulders, to the floor.

"Even so," she said, as though she had been reading my mind, "even this, it's not the worst thing in the world, is it?" she said as she cut. "When you get right down to it, everybody gets something out of it. We get our watermelons back, and everything that comes with it. Things are restored. Past is present again. And you — you get to be with a woman who wants to be with you. Honestly, though," she said, leaning down to whisper in my ear, "I was *shocked*. I never figured you for king material. After I saw you. A nice-looking boy and all. Good teeth. What's the problem?"

"There was no problem," I said. "It just never . . . felt right."

"So you've had girlfriends."

"Sure," I said.

"But you never felt it?"

"What?"

"*It*. Desire," she said, and she stopped cutting. Her hands rested on the top of my head, her fingers slowly moving. "Thoughtless, dark desire. It's the beginning of everything, of all life, the father and the mother, from the lowliest cell and bacterium to every boat leaving every harbor since the beginning of time, to the simplest-seeming, most awful little backwater town you can imagine to the most complex foundation of the world's greatest city. We do it, do what we want, and then, later, step back, and explain it, and decide if it was good or if it was bad, right or wrong, inspired or deluded. We are all the same that way."

She breathed deeply, and this breath of Ashland air seemed to bring her back to her dining room, to the present. She walked around to face me and looked me over closely.

"That's what you'll feel tonight," she said. "With the fire all around you, and every man and woman in town urging you on, you'll feel it inside you. And then a woman will come and take you through the fire itself and lead you away to a dark place, and it will all come pouring out."

I nodded. But I think she saw the fear in my eyes.

"It's not all that bad, Tom," she said. "What you'll be doing. It's not that bad at all."

I nodded again.

"It's how I met my husband," she said softly. "He was the king, and I was his queen. Maybe the same thing will happen to you." She ran her fingers through my hair. She pushed it back, over to one side.

"Where's Lucy?" I said.

"Where's Lucy?" she said. "What a question. Getting ready for the festival, of course. Like everybody else." She stepped back and looked me over. "I did pretty good for being nearly blind," she said.

She handed me a mirror, and I held it up before me. I recognized myself — who else would be there? — but it took a moment to reconcile the face in the mirror with the one I'd been used to seeing. My hair was short, and uneven, and a little spiky. Where it used to fall over the tops of my ears it was cut clean away, so I could see the perpendicular flap of my ears, the white flesh of my scalp behind and above them. My forehead was on display now too, and it was bigger than I'd ever imagined. All in all it was as though I'd been uncovered, and I could see myself for who I truly was. I looked like a boy from Ashland.

"Okay," she said. "Now for some clothes."

Mrs. Parsons disappeared for a minute and returned with an armload of shirts and pants, still on their hangers. She draped them across the back of a chair.

"Tom's," she said. "My husband's. Same as they were the day he died. Never could get rid of his clothes. How could I? They're still his, aren't they? Sometimes I just go through his closet, touching his shirts, remembering how they used to look on him. It's still there, his smell; just a hint of it. A mix of sweat and wood and tobacco. Do me this small favor," she said, "and wear them. For me, Tom? It'd go a long way to making me happy. And I've been good to you, haven't I? You've had a nice room, haven't you? Lucy and I, we've taken good care of you, haven't we?"

I looked at her. "Mrs. Parsons," I said. "I don't know. They're his clothes and he's —"

"Dead," she said. "But they're just clothes. Please?"

She left that I might get dressed in private.

"How lovely," she whispered when she returned, her eyes wide and misty. "You look so . . . *handsome* in that shirt, Tom. And those pants. Very nice. *Quite* the young gentleman."

"But, Mrs. Parsons," I said, standing in front of the dining room mirror. "This isn't me anymore."

"Nonsense," she said.

"My hair is too clipped and short. The shirt is tight. The pants just look like a big mistake. Those are my *ankles* down there. I can't let anyone see me like this."

But nothing I said got through to her at all.

"You don't know about love," she said.

"No," I said. "I don't."

"But you will learn."

In her hand was a bottle covered in dust; I could see where she had touched it because the dust had been rubbed away.

"Your cologne," she said, dripping some into her hand and smelling it, and drifting far, far away on its smell, before a moment passed and she came back to me. Then she rubbed it on my neck, her warm old hand lingering there, her eyes closed as if deep within a dream.

"Go," she said, leading me to the front door with her hands on my back, pushing as if I couldn't have found it myself. "Go, Tom. The women, they're waiting."

And they were. They were lined up along Main Street, in the shadows beneath the long awning. The sun peered down ferociously as I limped into town, dripping sweat. The women stood there, quietly, and watched. The world was almost too bright to see, the concrete's heat searing through the soles of my shoes. My back itched in places my hands couldn't reach. The clothes Mrs. Parsons had given me bit and pulled all over, and I walked with the stiff and unnatural movements of Frankenstein — which is what I felt like. I was a monster. As I passed in front of the plate-glass window of the hardware store, I saw myself, or what had become of myself, and I could feel the rage he felt over what he had been turned into, the lonely awfulness and the otherworldly terror of his hideousness.

The women smiled, shyly, and some laughed, their mouths behind their hands, as I walked down the street before them.

Hi Thomas, they said.

Morning, Thomas.

You're looking right nice today, Thomas.

Then they touched me. One by one their hands reached out and felt my head, my shoulders. One grabbed my arm and sunk her nails deep into my flesh, and I jerked my arm away and gasped, and she said, "He's tender." "Sensitive too," said another. The women were of every size, type, and age. Some were beautiful; some were not. Some were young, and some were not: grandmothers were there, and their granddaughters too, and they all touched me, pulling me back and forth between them, laughing now, almost singing, frenzied in their delight, until the line of women coalesced around me like metal filings to a magnet, and suddenly I was surrounded, unable to move, crushed between them, their bodies and their breasts and their legs, their sweat and their smell and their hands and the heat of the day choking me; they had sucked the air from my lungs and I was drowning, and I fell, escaping in the only way out left for me. I fainted.

I opened my eyes some time later, and all the women were gone. The street was empty and dead. Hours had passed. I was lying on a bench beneath the awning. Above me, slowly coming into focus, was Mr. Speegle. He smiled at me. He held the back of my head with his hand, and in the other a glass of cool water. I drank from it in sips.

"I think you're fine," he said. "I'm not a doctor, but I think you're doing fine."

"Thank you," I said.

"You've been out for a while," he said. "You missed the seed-spitting contest. I'm afraid you missed the seed count as well." I nodded, still drinking. "It broke a thousand," he said. "Everyone was surprised. A little boy won it." He smiled at me, his warm eyes crinkling behind his glasses. "And now, it's almost time." He nodded and held out my crown, the rounded end of a watermelon, hollowed out like a bowl, green on the outside, pink on the inside. "I cut it myself," he said. "It's my job as a member of the committee. Shall we see how it fits? You know, I've been waiting to do this for eighteen years. I think you could say I've been patient. And look at you," he said, placing the rind on my head and smiling. "Just look at you. It was worth the wait."

It is hard to describe the strange beauty of Ashland that night as I was pulled through the streets on the back of a cart by two horses, one black and one white, me sitting on a bale of hay beneath a big full moon, crowned, scepter in hand, waving at the solemn but expectant faces as I passed them by. Suddenly it all seemed to glow. The bright and starry sky, the torches of the townsfolk lining the way, and the distant small fires burning like beacons in the fields beyond. There was a rare summer wind. It was lovely. How had this happened? I wondered. How had Ashland become beautiful so suddenly? And then I understood. *This is the way it used to look.* When my mother came, and before the end of the watermelons, and history, and losing all they held dear, this is how Ashland appeared to its people, and that night I was able to see it through their eyes. This was the gift I was giving them by being the king. I was stunned by the power I had to deliver this to them, and this is what kept me there, standing on the cart.

By now, of course, I knew the routine. I had heard the story again and again from so many different people. I would be carried through town on the cart, where every man, woman, and child would stand on either side and look at me. And this is what happened, exactly. Some waved and smiled; others just stared. At my feet was a burlap sack. I reached into it, grabbed handfuls of dried watermelon seeds, and threw them out to everyone. The children darted into the street to collect them, but no one spoke or made a sound. The entire town was silent. The sound of the horses' hooves alone echoed down Main Street as the cart moved slowly past the courthouse and the square, to the edge of town, in the space between the last building and the dead, empty fields, where the horses stopped, and the wind blew warm all around me.

In the distance, out there in the blue dark, I could see three women in white. They were like silky ghosts, a dark efflorescence, just beyond the last lights of town. I stood on the back of the now still cart and watched them. This was the end, then. This is where I would truly become the king, Ashland's savior. I felt my heartbeat in my head. All that was left was for me to be taken from the cart and a ring of fire to be set all around me. Then, from the fields, a woman would come to me, she would walk through the fire and take my hand, and together the two of us would walk into the darkness, where she would have me, and I would have her. I would finally be a man. I waited for this to happen, alone.

But somehow I knew it wasn't going to happen that way when I saw it was Iggy who had come to take me from the cart. He was carrying an old red gasoline can. His limp had gotten worse since I'd seen him last. He'd been worked over again but good. A patch of blood stained his face.

"Hey, Thomas," he said.

"Iggy," I said.

Iggy looked at me, and suddenly I felt a little silly holding the old dried-up vine, my scepter, standing there with a watermelon rind on my head.

"What are you doing here, Iggy?" I said.

Iggy looked at me, and he smiled. He actually smiled, and I saw that he was missing a tooth.

"The fire," he said. "This year, I'm in charge of the fire."

"The fire?" I said.

He nodded and stuck out his hand. I took it and came down from the cart.

"You know," he said, "around you. Got to light it with something," he said, holding up the can. "I been pouring this stuff for a while. Kerosene. Since everybody cleared out for the parade. Smell it? It's happening right over here. See?"

A ring of kindling, about fifteen feet in diameter, lay a few yards into the first empty field. Iggy and I walked inside it and stood there side by side. The straw hut where the women were was farther out yet. The townspeople stayed a good distance away. I could see them over by the hardware store, glowing beneath their torches, which seemed to jump and shudder in the breeze. Some of the faces I knew: there was Mrs. Parsons and Betty Harris. There was Al Speegle and Carlton Snipes, and the little boy who had guessed how many seeds were in that watermelon, and there were some of the men who claimed they were my father. But my father wasn't here. My father was dead. His ashes were scattered here and there across the fields of his domain. He had flown into my eyes. I was at the end of a long line now, and there was no one else behind me. I was alone, and becoming scared of everything. I wanted it to be over, all of it. I turned to Iggy.

"Aren't you going to light it?" I asked him, because he and I had been standing there for some time, just broadcasting our vision all around us, looking at the shadows jumping on the buildings, and at each other.

He didn't seem to hear me at first. He just stood there, gazing. Then he looked across at me, and I could see his irises through the tiny slits of his eyes.

"Sure. I'm going to light it," he said. "But we need to take a minute, I think, to remember your mother."

He took a deep breath of air, and blinked a few times.

"I am just thinking about your mom," he said.

I nodded. She was something to remember now. Nothing real, but I had these stories. I had a lot of stories. I knew her better than I had before. I knew everyone better than I had before.

"I just wanted to be a normal man," he said. "She did everything she could to keep this from happening to me, and it killed her. She gave her life for *both* of us, Thomas — isn't that right? You and me both, we owe everything to her. Agree?"

And I nodded.

"I just wish I'd met her," I said.

He stuck out his hand.

"So let's shake. Good, then." He cleared his throat and his voice became deeper, proper. "It is in her memory, then, the memory of Lucy Rider, Thomas, your mother, my friend, that I have made myself in charge of this fire."

He reached into his pocket and took out a box of matches.

"You stay here," he said, "inside the ring," and he walked outside of it, and once there he turned and struck a match. His face glowed golden for an instant, then he kneeled down and laid it against the wood. Nothing happened, and for a moment I didn't think anything would. Then, with a *whoosh,* the circle of fire burst into life, and I was in the middle of it. It jumped, higher than I was, and quickly fell.

And then in the distance, I saw her. A white form moving closer. The woman who had captured the golden seed. I couldn't really make her out yet, couldn't see which one she was, but her gown was glowing like the moon as she walked through the dark fields. My hand shook as I held on to my scepter. I felt something dripping along one side of my face, but I couldn't tell if it was sweat or juice dribbling down from my crown. Iggy was still standing there at the edge of the ring, staring at me, then he looked over his shoulder, following my vision, and saw the girl. He shook his head and moved away, back to the edge of town, and then it was only the girl moving closer through the darkness and the townspeople chanting. I forgot to breathe. The fire rose steadily on its own. The woman came closer, but it was still dark. *She* was dark. The town seemed so far away now. There was nothing but the woman and the fire, and me inside the fire, waiting, sweating now, the blazing ring stinging me, like hot little needles in the air.

Lucy might not have actually walked through the fire, she may have done a little hop over it, but at that point I didn't care. Because here she was. A woman, the woman, for me.

"Ouch," she said.

She looked down at her bare feet, at the hem of her white dress. Nothing had caught fire.

"You okay?" I said.

"I'm okay," she said. "This is just a little scary." She looked around, as though she expected something, some difference in the world inside the ring. She seemed a little disappointed that there wasn't, that there was only me. Then she held out her hand.

"The golden seed," she said.

"The price of admission," I said, and I looked at it, and at her.

"Yeah," she said. "I went for it. Knocked those white girls out of the way. Made a grab. Came up lucky."

She smiled and winked at me. And she had a pleasing smile. Everything she did was pleasing, it seemed to me then. When she crossed her arms and shook her head, something about it, about even the smallest move, was just beautiful to look at, and it made me feel dizzy. Lucy was like a kind of good news — she gave me that feeling. Then she walked up to me and looked me hard in the eye. Didn't blink.

"I'm here," she said. "And I'm here because I want to be. But I . . . I don't know that I can do this, what we're supposed to do right now."

"Me either," I said, relieved.

"We don't have to," she said.

"Nope," I said.

"We're not bound by anything," she said. "Not anymore. You think they'd have let me be here if they'd had a choice?" She smiled. "This is all new. We don't have to do anything we don't want to."

"Let's don't and say that we did," I said.

"How would they know?"

"If we both say the same thing," I said. "If we both stick to our stories."

"Okay," she said. "What's our story? That's what we have to figure out."

As we tried to talk ourselves out of doing what we came here to do, we drew closer, and I felt her breasts brush against my chest, and then we pulled back, but only slightly.

"You smell good," I said.

"Like smoke."

"Good smoke," I said. "Like good smoke."

"I don't even know you," she said softly. "You don't know me."

"It's weird," I said. "And you never?"

"No," she said. "You?"

"Never," I said.

"Two people should know each other before," she said. "Especially the first time."

"That's what I think," I said.

"Good."

"Then why did you come?" I said.

"I don't know," she said, thinking about it. "I felt like I had to. I felt like — it's hard to explain — that there was nowhere else I could be. You're not a part of this town. Neither am I. I figured we could get out together."

And I kissed her, without even knowing what I was doing or that I was going to do it. I kissed her, and she let me. My arms held her close and she held me tight herself. It wasn't just us now either — that's the way it felt to me. Suddenly we were under some spell, in the groove of history, surrounded by something important.

I took off my shirt and unbuttoned my pants. Lucy stepped back and slipped the straps from her shoulders, slowly, one by one, and her gown fell, and the moment it did, my eyes full, her sweet dark body brilliant in the firelight, the world came to an end. Or it seemed to. Ashland burst into a sudden flame. It was as though a huge bomb had exploded. The ground rumbled and shook and cracked. For a moment the night sky was as bright as day, for Ashland itself had become like the sun. From one end of Main Street to the other, the entire town suddenly began to burn, to glow, to sizzle and explode. This, I realized, was the fire Iggy had in mind all along. A trail of it led to the little red gasoline cans he used to fill up his lawn mower. They would end up as bombs of flame.

"Oh," she said, "Thomas."

"I know," I said. "What should we do? The whole town's on fire."

"Not that," she said, and I looked at her, and she wasn't watching the town. She was staring at me. We were both naked now. The town behind us was burning, and she was looking at me. So I looked at me too.

"Oh."

"Yeah. What I said," she said. "Oh."

After that, we didn't know what to say or what to do. She came a little closer. Then she smiled, and her eyes narrowed, and she reached out tentatively with her hand, and she looked up.

"It's okay," I said.

And then she touched it, and in a heartbeat jumped back, because that was all it took, her touch, this first time, and I came pouring out all over. I felt sorry for a second, bad for her and for myself, and almost said I was, but then I knew I shouldn't be, because this was what was meant to happen. We both seemed to know it. She laughed, moving backwards, looking at the dirt where it had fallen, because suddenly, right there, the dead ground itself began to move, and out of it came the curious ends of tendrils, eagerly swirling and snaking now all around us, to the edge of the fire and back, vine after vine, conscious and alive, some hardy and thick enough to break through the ring itself and burrow into the dark fields around us. Soon the entire patch of ground was covered, so thick with vines we could have laid down on them like a bed.

Behind us, the chanting had stopped, and, in the distance, high voices and a terrible screaming began. I could see the crowd scatter like animals, dropping their torches in panic, which only spread the fire further. I had never seen anything so awful, or so wonderful, at the same time. The whole town glowed, gloriously, and Iggy stood there, alone against the wall of firelight, gazing at it proudly. Then he turned to me and waved, like a little boy. *Look what I've done!* he was saying. *Look at what I've made!*

The ring of fire grew higher still, but the spell was broken. Lucy picked up her gown, and I pulled my pants and shirt from the tangle of the vines. People ran past us in the night, dark figures. No one seemed to care about us now, and what we were supposed to be doing. Someone stopped at the edge of the ring, his face glowing red, watching us. It was Carlton Snipes. I saw him clearly. He came walking through the fire that surrounded us. He took his time. The cuffs of his slacks were smoldering by the time he got through the ring, and smoky, but I couldn't tell if it had burned him, or if he'd even noticed it if it had, or that any fire would have kept him back. The side of his face was blackened with ash. A streak of sweat cut through the ash on his face and left a clear trail down his withered cheek. He glanced at Lucy without an ounce of feeling in his eyes. He looked at the green vines all around his feet. Then he looked at me, and he walked up to me, glaring at me with a pure hatred. He knocked the crown off my head with one hand and grabbed me by the collar of my shirt with the other, pulling me close to his dark eyes, strong and hard for an old man.

"First it was your mother killing our crops," he said, his voice rigid with rage. "But that wasn't enough. You had to do *this*." And he raised his hands into the air, indicating everything around us, everything burning and falling apart, as if it were my fault.

"Why, son?" he said. "Why? Nobody ever asked you to come here; nobody asked *her*. I mean, what did we ever do, anyway? We're not bothering anybody. Why can't you people just *leave us alone*?"

As he spoke these last words he grabbed me by the throat and held me there, strangling me. I tried to knock his arm away, but it was hard, like metal, and I was weak. I couldn't breathe. I felt the blood pulsing in my brain, the sound of it in my ears, until Lucy, looking out for me now, knocked him on the side of his head with one powerful jolt from her fist, and he fell to the ground, on his knees, his eyes full of tears and pain and begging for whatever mercy we had.

"How dare you?" she said. "Treating a king that way."

And that's how we left him, on his knees in the fire, the watermelon vines coiling around his ankles and legs, thinking, if thought is what it was, that any sacrifice was better than none at all.

So. The town burned down. All of it. All of their history and mine too — for what it was worth — gone now. Iggy, Mrs. Parsons, Al Speegle, Sugar, the Old Man, Jonah Carpenter, Betty Harris, Vincent Newby, Terry Smith, and all the rest of them weren't homeless — their homes were still there — but they were townless now. When Lucy and I left that night it was still burning, and what wasn't burning was being covered over by vines. You could see it from the highway in the distance, the embers glowing eerily through the pines, a brand-new ruin-in-the-making.

We were quiet, driving away. I glanced in the rearview mirror occasionally, but Lucy didn't look back once; she just stared ahead and didn't say a word. The hum of the road beneath the car wheels was the only sound. We drove down the hill, past the gas station, and sped up when we hit Highway 31, going south. I looked back again and the light from the town had disappeared. We were really gone. There were other cars on the highway, other people from other towns, and we were just another one, driving down the road at night. The car began to shudder as the speedometer hit sixty, but it always had. It was an old American car that had once belonged to my father. This was the car he drove to Ashland himself, eighteen years ago. He'd gotten another car since then — Anna drove it now — but he'd kept this one because he thought it would be a good starter car, for when I turned sixteen. And he was right — it was.

"Lucy?" I said, after a while.

She looked at me and smiled. Still, I could tell she was shy. Even after everything we'd been through — maybe especially after everything we'd been through — she was shy. "Yes, Thomas?" she said.

"Nothing," I said, and shook my head.

"Nothing?" she said. "Really?"

"Yeah, I mean — it's nothing."

"What?" she said. "Come on. Tell me."

I changed lanes; someone needed to pass me. "No, it's — I was just wondering — can you hear that?"

And Lucy said, "What?"

"The car," I said. "It's making a sound."

She listened for a minute. "Okay," she said, nodding. "Yep. I hear it. It's like a — *swoosh, swoosh, swoosh.*"

"Not that sound," I said. "It always makes that sound. There's another one. Kind of a *kriiink, kriiink.* Listen."

So we stopped talking, and she listened for the sound. I could tell she was listening by the way her face became so still, and her eyes opened wide but didn't focus on anything, and she didn't even blink until she stopped listening and looked at me and said, "I don't hear it, Thomas."

I shrugged my shoulders.

"It's probably nothing," I said.

"Probably," she said, nodding.

Then she put her bare feet flush against the dash, and with her legs in the air her gown draped over her knees like a tent. We passed a sign that said BIRMINGHAM 57 MILES. I still had the clothes on Mrs. Parsons had given me. I still had the note Lucy had written in my pocket. *Welcome to our lovely town.* And Lucy still had the golden seed. It was in the palm of her hand, and she was staring at it. She was staring at it like doing that was going to help her figure something out. But I knew it wouldn't, and I wanted to tell her so.

"Lucy," I said. "Listen —"

But she held up her hand then, to make me quiet. The seed was resting in the palm of the other. Her body moved forward, and her eyes were wide open, and then her face broke into a picture of perfect brightness as if, suddenly, everything was clear to her.

"*Yes,*" she said then.

"What?" I said. "Yes what?"

"There, Thomas. Hear it? I can hear it now. The sound. But it's kind of a *ka-ching, ka-ching, ka-ching,* isn't it? Kind of?"

We listened to the sound together, as though it were a song.

"It's a *ka-ching,*" I said. "Definitely a *ka-ching.*"

She looked at me.

"Are *ka-ching*s dangerous?" she said.

"Sometimes."

"But this one doesn't sound too dangerous to me."

"I think you're right," I said. "This is a good one. This is a good *ka-ching.*"

And from that moment on time seemed to fly, and we were home before we knew it.

FOUR

And yea one supon a time it is ritten, a child will be born in this town, call it Ashland, and he will have nuthin a tall.

Hole parts of him will be missin. His looks will be not much to look at. Ugly as a dog, this child.

His own Ma and daddy will die in a car crash.

Wats more sad, they wont be much to miss.

He is in lass place in life. Persons can look at him and yea, this is wat they see, the n of the line, cause he will have nuthin a tall. He wont no anything ether. He wont no *when two vowels go walking, the first one does the talking.*

That will cum later.

For a woman will cum to town and give him the thing he need to no.

When you eat "dessert," you always want to cum back for the second "s."

And other things.

But like all of the good, she to will go.

Yea, she will give every thing for the child who has nuthin. She will die giving life. Time past and past agin. And her boy will cum, and it is all the same. Agin. No change a tall.

If you thnk things change you arnt lookin at the rite things.

So. I brot the fire. An nuthin is everwhere now. Its just me and nuthin elks, and that is a lot of nuthin.

But a good thing to, cause now we can start all over.

Fresh.

New and Improved.

OK.

One supon a time all over agin. One supon a time.

Iggy